Highland Laddie Gone

**Center Point
Large Print**

**This Large Print Book carries the
Seal of Approval of N.A.V.H.**

ॐ श्री गणेशाय नमः

Highland Laddie Gone

Sharyn McCrumb

Center Point Publishing
Thorndike, Maine • USA

Bolinda Publishing
Melbourne • Australia

To Gavin
Whose advice and inspiration I needed . . .
More than Wisdom or a Drink

This Center Point Large Print edition is published in the year 2002
by arrangement with Ballantine Publishing Group,
a division of Random House, Inc.

This Bolinda Large Print edition is published in the year 2002
by arrangement with Ballantine Publishing Group,
a division of Random House, Inc.

The text of this Large Print edition is unabridged. In other aspects, this book
may vary from the original edition. Printed in Thailand. Set in 16-point
Times New Roman type by Bill Coskrey and Gary Socquet.

US ISBN 1-58547-213-1
BC ISBN 1-74030-755-0

U.S. Library of Congress Cataloging-in-Publication Data.

McCrumb, Sharyn, 1948-
    Highland laddie gone / Sharyn McCrumb.--Center Point large print ed.
    p. cm.
    ISBN 1-58547-213-1 (lib. bdg. : alk. paper)
    1. MacPherson, Elizabeth (Fictitious character)--Fiction. 2. Women forensic
anthropoligists--Fiction. 3. Americans--Scotland--Fiction. 4. Highland games--Fiction.
5. Scotland--Fiction. 6. Large type books. I. Title.

PS3563.C3527 H54 2002
813'.54--dc21

2002020087

Australian Cataloguing-in-Publication.

McCrumb, Sharyn, 1948-
Highland laddie gone / Sharyn McCrumb.
ISBN 1740307550
1. Large type books.
2. Women forensic anthropologists--Fiction.
3. Mystery fiction.
I. Title.
813.54

British Cataloguing-in-Publication is available from the British Library.

Here's tae us. Wha's like us—
damn few an' they're a' deid.
　　　　　　—Traditional Scots toast

AUTHOR'S NOTE

When I am not writing mysteries I am a regional scholar, and as such I am particularly concerned with cultural patterns, dialect, etc. Therefore, when I decided to have three Scots as main characters in this book, I consulted the real thing. Dr. Gavin Faulkner, who turned out to be Scotland's answer to Henry Higgins, guided me through hours of research, provided invaluable material on dialects, and even went along to a few Highland games to test my cultural theories. I couldn't have done it without him.

I am also grateful to Dr. Alan Haddow (Colonel Pickering to Gavin's Higgins) for being more help to a writer than one could reasonably expect of an engineer, and to Marcia Romano and Stephen Goldie for their help with Glaswegian. The Scots-Americans at the various Highland festivals have without exception been friendly and helpful to me in researching my book—even the Campbells. Most of the aberrations depicted herein are purely imaginary, but the cultural observations are as accurate as I was able to make them.

Glencoe Mountain Games

WESTERN VIRGINIA'S OWN SCOTTISH FESTIVAL
LABOR DAY WEEKEND

SCHEDULE OF EVENTS
Scottish Field Events
Highland Parade of Clans
Dancing & Piping Competitions
Clan Hospitality Tents
Ceilidh (Scottish Pub & Dancing)
Border Collie Herding Events
Scottish Items for Sale
Glencoe Festival Craft Fair

Camping Facilities and Some Motel Accommodations

FOR INFORMATION:
Dr. G. Andrew Carson
Glencoe Mountain Games Chairman
7091 Bonnie Bell Drive
Meadow Creek, Virginia

Or: Your Local Scottish Heritage Society

THE SOUTHERN HIGHLANDER NEWSLETTER

A Wee Word From Heather McSkye

Lots of exciting Do's to share with you this month! Gregory Spence (the dashing dermatologist who looks *divine* in a kilt) is whisking off to the auld country for a well-earned vacation. We'll miss you at the games, Greg!

Jeff and Bitsy Lockerby (of White Oak Farms) are the proud parents of a wee bairn, Bonnie Jean, born July 25th. Congratulations to Clan Douglas on a new addition!

A tip of the tam to Taylor McKinnon for winning first prize in country dancing at North Carolina Highland Games. (Can you believe that Babs and Ed have a college-age daughter?)

Speaking of Highland games, SCOTS WHAT HAE . . . the time and energy should be getting ready for next month's Virginia Gala. This will be my first festival as a member of Clan MacDonald and I'm as nervous as a corbie on a high road! My husband Batair (that's Gaelic for Walter; and he's Dr. Hutcheson to his patients) is an old hand at this festival business, since he is in his second term as clan chief. He has arranged for Clan MacDonald to have its own tent at the games.

BRING YOUR OWN GLENLIVET!—A special thanks to that dear Betty Carson (so organized!) for heading up the hospitality committee. I'll be on hand to help her out—any more volunteers out there?

Batair and I were among the guests at Doug and Paige Stewart's anniversary party last week. After a lovely dinner of prime rib, set on a table fit for the Bonnie Prince, we all went in to Paige's stunning Queen Anne living room and watched slides of their trip to Scotland. They didn't get to my old home place, but I've made them promise to visit it on their next trip.—Thanks to all the Highlanders here for making a newcomer to the country—and a newlywed— feel so welcome!

Note: Those with questions about the border collie herding competition, please don't ask me! I'm completely bewildered by all creatures great and small. The person you need to talk to is the *first* Mrs. Walter Hutcheson, who can be reached at . . .

CLAN CHATTAN

Dear Elizabeth,

How are you? It's been ages! Due to a security leak in your organization (your mom), I have obtained your address and am writing to ask a favor. (In business school they teach us to come to the point in the first paragraph.) Did you know that I'm getting my MBA at Princeton! The folks are so thrilled about it—Daddy's plastered bumper stickers on every vehicle we own, *even* the riding lawn mower. It's quite sweet, really, to see them so happy. Your mother didn't say what you were doing.

Haven't seen you at the Highland games festivals since high school. You really ought to come to one. Surely you're not still upset about the dance competition. Goodness, there's so much more to a festival than that! There's the hospitality tent, and the nametag chairman. Not everybody is meant to be graceful, you know.

Anyway, I hope I can persuade you to come to the Labor Day games (see enclosed brochure), because there is something that I need a volunteer for. You remember Cluny, don't you? He's fine, as reserved as ever. For the past two years, I've been the person in charge of him for the festivals. You know how they like a pretty girl to show him off. Well, this year I simply can't come! I'll be in Europe during term break with my flatmate. So, I need someone to take my place. Buffy and Pax and Cammie-Lynn were all booked up, so I'm hoping that you'll show the old Clan spirit and volunteer for the job. But if you can't afford it, do say so, and I'll understand.

Please let me know soon about this. I'm off to Europe next week. Oh, and what have you been doing lately? Teaching?

Got to run!

Mary-Stuart Gillespie

Dear Mary-Stuart,

⋅ Can't tell you how devastated I am to hear that you won't be at the Highland games this year. In that case, I guess I'll go. And I'll be happy to take care of Cluny. He's my favorite member of Clan Chattan, anyway.

No, I'm not teaching. I'm getting a degree in forensic anthropology, along with my fiancé, Milo Gordon. We spend a lot of time cutting up dead bodies. I think of you often.

Sincerely,
Elizabeth

CHAPTER ONE

"There! I told you we weren't lost!" said Elizabeth MacPherson, slapping the steering wheel. "Look at the bumper sticker on that car."

Her cousin Geoffrey assumed an expression of world-weary disdain. "The one that says: Do it with a Piper?"

"Yes. Meaning bagpipes. They must be on their way to the Scottish festival."

"Or perhaps to an exterminators' convention. One can but hope," sighed Geoffrey.

"You promised you were going to behave," Elizabeth reminded him.

"If our theatre group weren't producing *Brigadoon* next spring, you would never have got me to come."

"I know, Geoffrey," said Elizabeth sweetly. "But you were my second choice for someone to go with."

"Oh? And who was your first choice?"

Elizabeth shrugged. "Just anybody."

She continued to follow the blue station wagon along Virginia Highway 42, looking for signs announcing the Western Virginia Highland Games. Why did I want someone to come with me, Elizabeth wondered. Is it a holdover from the old days when a woman alone was a wallflower? She stole a glance at Geoffrey, who had gone back to reading the playscript. She had better make some effort to stay on good terms with him for the weekend: Geoffrey was known for his skill at subtle revenge.

"It will be nice to have you along," she admitted. "These Scottish gatherings tend to be mostly families and old men.

Unattached young men will be at a premium."

Geoffrey struck a pose. "Young men like me would be at a premium in *heaven,* my dear."

Elizabeth nodded. "There will be very few of you there, if that's what you mean."

"It sounds like a senior citizens' costume party. Whatever did you want to come for?"

"It can be a lot of fun. I used to come every year until I went off to college. Once I got third place in the country dancing."

"Just the two of you competing, I suppose?" asked Geoffrey solemnly.

Elizabeth sighed. "Should we keep score this weekend?"

"I think not. Your best bet is an unconditional surrender. Now, to get back to this Highland fling you've dragged me to: I hope I am not expected to wear a kilt."

"No. Lots of people wear ordinary clothes."

"I could never be accused of that," Geoffrey assured her, smoothing his yellow poplin slacks. "That reminds me. I did bring along something to get into the spirit of things."

He reached into the pocket of his navy blue blazer and drew out a red and green plaid necktie. "There! Now, how do you say *tacky* in Gaelic?"

Elizabeth glanced at the tie, swerved the car, and fixed her eyes firmly on the road again. "You're not going to wear that," she informed him.

"Why not? I thought it was rather fetching. Though not perhaps with yellow slacks."

"It's the Royal Stewart tartan, Geoffrey."

He clutched the tie to his chest. "Possession is nine-tenths of the law!"

"Idiot. I mean, it's the plaid of the Scottish royal family. No one but them is supposed to wear it."

"Then there must be an awful lot of them, because I see it on stadium blankets, dog coats—"

"I know, but remember that this is a Scottish festival, where they enforce rules like that. At least, Dr. Campbell does."

"Who?"

"If we're lucky he won't be here this year. But I doubt if wild horses could keep him away. He's the president of the local chapter of Clan Campbell, and he is the most exasperating old grouch alive! He's a stickler for Scottish etiquette, and an absolute bore about family trees."

"Not unlike yourself, in fact," Geoffrey observed.

"You are not wearing that tie, Geoffrey," Elizabeth replied calmly. "If you want to join in, you can wear a MacPherson tie; or you can find out if the Chandlers were affiliated with any clan; but wear the Royal Stewart you may not. I won't be seen with anyone doing that. Or wearing Campbell colors, of course."

"What are Campbell colors? Purple and orange?"

"The tartan, I mean. You can't be a Campbell. Honestly, I don't know why they even come to these gatherings."

"They sound marvelous," said Geoffrey, with the first trace of interest he had thus far displayed. "Do they kidnap children? Dip snuff? Play acid rock on their bagpipes?"

Elizabeth was so distracted by this last possibility that she nearly forgot to answer. "Of course not," she finally said. "They were on the wrong side, that's all. It's like going to a Civil War reenactment and being a Yankee."

"Does this have something to do with Bonnie Prince

Charlie—he of my forbidden necktie?" asked Geoffrey, fingering the object in question.

"Of course. In 1745 the Highland clans backed Charles Edward Stuart against the Hanovers for the throne of England. He raised an army in Scotland, and—"

"The MacPhersons were on his side, I take it?"

"Naturally."

"And the Campbells . . . weren't?" Geoffrey beamed with pride at the magnitude of his deduction.

"Right. The final battle was at Culloden in 1746. The Highland clans with swords and an inoperative cannon stood against the British army *and* the Campbells, who were armed with muskets and bayonets!"

Geoffrey blinked. "There seems to be nothing wrong with the Campbells' *intelligence,* then. The MacPhersons, on the other hand—"

"It was a massacre," said Elizabeth, ignoring him. "And *after* the battle, the Duke of Cumberland's army spent months in the Highlands, killing every man, woman, and child they could find. They virtually obliterated the Highland clans."

"Hardly that," Geoffrey protested. "Judging from these Scottish gatherings, I'd say you were all breeding like hamsters."

"We're the refugees," snapped Elizabeth, glossing over a few centuries. "The ones who could escaped to Ireland, and then to America or Canada."

Geoffrey nodded comprehension. "I see! But, Elizabeth, what are the Campbells doing here then? Shouldn't they all be back in Scotland, living it up, having the place all to themselves?"

Elizabeth was shaken by this hitherto unconsidered question. "Never mind about that!" she muttered. "They're probably all descended from younger sons who got booted out to the colonies."

"That's right," smiled Geoffrey. "I'd forgotten that everyone in Virginia is descended from the English nobility. Not a yeoman in the state."

Elizabeth made a face at him.

"With all that fiction going around, I don't see why I couldn't be a Royal Stewart. Wasn't Bonnie Prince Charlie called The Pretender? It fits right in."

"Forget it, Geoffrey."

"You are so unreasonable. You won't even indulge me in my one bit of whimsy, when I have been a perfect saint about putting up with *your* eccentricity."

Geoffrey turned around and stared meaningfully at the passenger in the backseat, who returned the glare with malevolent yellow eyes.

CHAPTER TWO

"Poor Cluny!" cried Elizabeth, glancing again into the rearview mirror. "Does he look hungry?"

"He's gazing longingly at my throat," said Geoffrey. "It may not be the same thing."

"We'd better feed him. Can you reach that cooler on the floor of the backseat?"

"With my *hand*?"

"I can't believe that he would condescend to bite you, but I'll stop the car anyway."

Cluny, the clan mascot, was a regal bobcat who

embodied the Chattan motto: *Touch Not the Cat*. He lounged on the backseat, wearing a tartan ribbon over his metal collar, and a look of heavy-lidded insolence. Several times a year, Cluny's owner lent him out to attend Scottish festivals, where he enjoyed overeating and sneering at the antics of the primates. Since Cluny was declawed and had never found anyone worth the energy to bite, he was generally believed to be tame, but his expression of cordial dislike kept most admirers at bay. "My ancestors used to eat your ancestors," he seemed to be thinking behind his yellow stare.

Elizabeth stopped the car on a level stretch of grass beside the road. "Poor pussums," she cooed. "Is-ums hungry?"

Cluny yawned and flexed a paw against the upholstery. "I wish you had been that solicitous when I wanted to stop and eat," Geoffrey remarked.

"Get the cooler out of the backseat," said Elizabeth. "I'll walk him around."

Geoffrey hoisted the plastic ice chest, which was heavier than he expected, and deposited it ungently on the grass. "What's in this thing? Judge Crater?"

"The bobcat bill of fare for the entire weekend. All I have to do is keep adding ice to the cooler—and there should be lots of that around, considering how those doctors drink. Come on, Cluny, din-din." She opened the box. "Let's see what we have here. How about ground chuck?"

"As opposed to Geoffrey Tartare," murmured Geoffrey, edging out of the way.

"He must be very expensive to feed," Elizabeth remarked as Cluny inhaled a fist-size chunk of meat.

"Consider the alternative."

"Dry cat food?"

"Door-to-door salesmen, Jehovah's Witnesses . . ."

"I keep telling you, he's not dangerous. Just a little reserved. I hope he'll get along with dogs. Marge may be there."

Geoffrey smiled. "Does she know what you think of her?"

"What? . . . Oh, I see. What I meant was that Marge Hutcheson always brings border collies to the games, and I wouldn't want them to chase Cluny. Or vice versa. Marge was always one of my favorite people at the games. I used to help her set up the gates and ramps for the herding competition."

"Do you mean to tell me there will be sheep at this ordeal?" asked Geoffrey, inspecting the sole of his shoe as if anticipating future indignities.

"No. Of course, in Scotland border collies herd sheep; but for the games here, sheep are too much trouble to haul around, so most exhibitors use ducks. It's amazing what the dogs can get those ducks to do."

"Oh, I don't know. I'll bet if we got a giant carnivore to slink around after you, you'd be doing amazing things, too." He paused to look at Elizabeth, who was hopping on one foot with one hand arched over her head.

"I'm shedding," she informed him, placing her left foot in front of her knee, then behind it, then in front again.

"A balsam conditioner would do you a world of good, but why are you bouncing around like that?"

Elizabeth pretended to stop in order to answer his question, and Geoffrey pretended not to see her gasping for breath. "Shedding," she said between heaves. "Name of . . . dance step . . . Highland fling . . . practicing."

"You're not going to practice too much, are you, dear? Father insisted that we learn CPR, but it's been *years*."

"Dinna worry about me, laddie!" snapped Elizabeth.

"Oh, now really, this is too much! I can take the costumes and the peculiar dancing, but if you start lapsing into a vaudeville Scottish burr, I will lock you in the trunk for the duration of the festival."

"You're not going to be any fun at all."

"Nonsense! I shall be indispensable. With all those demented hams running around pretending to be Jacobites, I shall be that all-important figure: the audience. I expect to enjoy myself hugely."

"You'll be lucky if no one brains you with a bagpipe," muttered Elizabeth.

Dr. Colin Campbell glared at the gaggle of pipe-band members trying to dash across the road to the cafe, apparently trusting their youth and stamina to transport them before his Winnebago mowed them down. They couldn't be presuming on Dr. Campbell's good-will: the nonexistence of *that* was an accepted fact among the games crowd.

Just what you'd expect of a Campbell, most people said, thereby overlooking an important psychological point. Highland games festivals spent a lot of time emphasizing Scottish traditions and lauding Bonnie Prince Charlie, whose band of overconfident nincompoops were slaughtered, sword in hand, by the musket-toting Campbells. To the idealists enamored of lost causes, coming to a battle well fed, with state-of-the-art weaponry and a sizable army to back you up, was cheating; and the Campbells were vilified in song and jest for their calculating and unsportsmanlike behavior. Some two hundred and forty-odd years after the Battle of Culloden, the Campbells were still considered the flies in the broth of Scotland, which explains why Colin Campbell thrived on ill will. What other sort of person would go, year after year, to a gathering at which he was guaranteed to be hated?

Dr. Campbell waited until he could see the whites of the pipe band's eyes before pumping his horn, which blared out, "The Campbells are coming! Hooray! Hooray!" As he sped off in the direction of the campsite, he could see them in his rearview mirror shaking their fists and shouting Campbell epithets. Colin smiled; it was an auspicious beginning for the games.

Jerry Buchanan winced as he removed his kilt from the monogrammed clothes bag. Whoever had inquired "What's in a name?" had not been a Buchanan of Scottish origin. In Scotland, last names denote clan affiliation, and thereby clan tartan, which meant that Jerry Buchanan would spend a lifetime of Highland festivals running around in a tartan of red, green, and yellow with a predominant orange stripe, in marked contrast to the muted grays and browns he wore the rest of the time. Why couldn't he have been a Gordon or a Douglas, with their tasteful blues and greens?

Jerry was tired of having to be good-natured about the jokes—that Barnum and Bailey were septs of Clan Buchanan; that Buchanan was Gaelic for *rainbow.* He'd almost rather be a Campbell. He had considered quitting the games circuit, but he did enjoy the sporting events, and he had quite a reputation as a hurler. The trophies looked good in his office waiting room, and it gave him something in common with MacDonald and Ogilvy, his partners at the clinic. Someday it might even be worth more than that.

Jerry glanced out the window to see if a battered old AirStream had pulled into the campgrounds yet. Someday all this Highland business might pay off very well indeed, he told himself. Jerry didn't usually dabble in politics, but this was different. He wondered what news would be arriving with the man in the AirStream. Perhaps he would speak to him about changing the Buchanan colors—when he had the power to do it, of course. When he was the Earl of Buchanan.

Jerry smiled, picturing his little dental office tucked into the turret of a castle and his receptionist decked out in a kilt of tasteful blue and gray.

Cameron Dawson hadn't said anything for six miles, ever since he had realized that nobody was going to talk about porpoises; but his hosts hadn't noticed his silence. Probably never would, at the rate they were nattering about this festival they were taking him to. From what he could gather, they all thought it was the most amazing stroke of good fortune that their visiting professor from Scotland had arrived just as the Highland festival was about to begin: it solved the problem of how to entertain him for the weekend.

Cameron Dawson was less sanguine about the coincidence: he would have preferred to be given a tour of fast-food restaurants and then left alone with a big-screen color television hooked up to cable. But it was not to be. He wasn't sure just what to expect of an American Scottish festival, but if the previous hour's conversation was any example, it was going to be the longest weekend of Cameron Dawson's life.

"You're sure you don't have a kilt, Dr. Dawson?" asked Mrs. Carson with a disbelieving smile.

"Positive," said Cameron, trying to smile back. *And you're sure you don't wrestle alligators?* he wanted to answer.

"Dawson—what clan is that, anyway?" asked Andy Carson, the assistant dean of biology. Opinions in the department were divided over whether he had taken up the study of salamanders because he looked like one, or whether he had grown to resemble them after long years of close association.

"Clan MacThatcher," said Cameron, going for broke. Betty Carson giggled. "You can't fool us! There's no such clan. I'll look you up." She held up a small book called *Scottish Clans and Tartans*, which Cameron realized he was expected to know by heart. "Dawson . . . Dawson . . ." she murmured, flipping pages. "Ah, here it is! 'Dawson is a corruption of Davidson, and the Davidsons are now a branch of Clan Chattan.' I'll turn you over to one of them for the parade of clans. I expect you'll want to be with your clan, won't you?"

Cameron blinked. "Do any of them know anything about porpoises?"

Betty Carson considered it. "If they're like most clans, they'll be M.D.s. Andy always introduces himself as Professor Carson, rather than Doctor, so that people won't try to talk to him about AMA politics."

"Or tax shelters," Andy Carson grunted. "They certainly prescribe good Scotch, though, at these festivals. What's your brand, Scotty?"

"Schweppes," murmured Cameron. He'd be damned if he'd be called Scotty for the duration of his stay. If they persisted, he'd have to think up a nickname "that they called him back home."

"Well, maybe they'll let you enter the sporting events without the kilt," said Betty Carson. "Since you're a real Scot. Is there any particular one you specialize in?"

"Soccer." He remembered not to call it football.

She frowned. "Not Scottish. The choices are caber toss, sheaf toss, hammer toss, stone throw—"

"Betty won the haggis hurl last year," said her husband proudly.

Cameron tried to imagine a group of women vomiting suet pudding in a distance competition. That couldn't be it.

Ice. Americans were really quite demented on the subject of ice, thought Heather McSkye.

While her new husband, Dr. Hutcheson, was conferring with festival officials, Heather climbed into the camper to check on the ice supply. She had filled the cooler before they left, but in this stifling climate it might have melted; and if so, she would have to send Batair to town for more. He would insist on having the other clan chiefs in for drinks tonight, and they would need more ice than a fish-monger to accommodate that crowd.

Usually Heather enjoyed entertaining: sheathed in a black dress to accentuate her blondness, she would glide among the guests, murmuring introductions or offers of drinks, and accepting compliments on the newly redecorated house. Batair had protested, of course—men are such sticks about change—but she had told him she simply couldn't live with Marge's old chintzes and cottage oak antiques. She'd wanted to hold a yard sale, but Batair, in an uncharacteristic display of firmness, insisted on sending the old furniture to Marge at the farm. He hadn't even wanted to readjust the settlement to compensate for it. The divorce agreement had allowed Marge to keep their farm, where she raised her border collies, and Dr. Hutcheson had kept the house in town and most of the stocks and bonds.

Heather would have liked to see more acrimony in the relations between her husband and his first wife, but she was too clever to instigate it. She contented herself with the purchase of some lovely chrome and glass furniture to complement the scarlet settee and the black pile carpet. Batair seemed to think that, since she was from Scotland, she should be as daft about antiques as he was, but it wasn't as if she'd grown up in a sodding castle, then, was it? Heather liked new things; in fact, she would have preferred motor racing to Scottish games for entertainment, but the games were not entertainment as far as she was concerned. They were a means to an end.

She had sized up the Scots-Americans and decided that they were the U.S. equivalent of the Sloanes back home: conservative snobs with more money than sense, in search of a bit of antiquity on which to hang their pedigrees. When Heather mentioned her ties to the Scottish nobility, Batair had practically drooled, hadn't he? If the other Americans' reactions were as funny as that, it should be an amusing weekend indeed.

James Stuart McGowan hadn't said anything for quite a long time; but since he was only ten years old, his parents considered that a blessing. Even an ominous silence was better than the leveling remarks that were his usual conversational contributions on outings.

James Stuart, who had the soul of an aging Baptist minister, had been cursed with whimsical parents. They were always trying to drag him off to carnivals and ball games, where they'd buy noxious quantities of hot dogs and cotton candy that they attempted to pass off as dinner; God knows what this cuisine had done to his metabolism. If his parents didn't get a grip on themselves by the time he reached puberty, he'd probably die of terminal acne. At least he'd gotten them to stop swiping his copy of Nietzsche and replacing it with *Paddington Bear*; the threat to call the child protection agency had finally done it. He wondered which of his parents had put the sign on his door: *Killjoy was here.*

This latest obsession of theirs, the Highland games, appeared to involve leaving a perfectly comfortable home to camp out like gypsies on the top of a mountain amid bears, poison oak, and fellow psychotics. His mother and father (he steadfastly refused to call them Babs and Stewie) even wanted to buy a kilt for him, insisting how adorable he'd look in the family tartan. James Stuart had countered by demanding to see the family checkbook, and pointing out that $150 worth of cuteness was clearly beyond their means.

Although he felt obliged to radiate displeasure at his parents' latest escapade, James Stuart secretly felt that the Highland games might prove interesting after all. There should be crowds of people there, so that he could easily give his parents the slip and stay gone for hours. Besides, feeling superior and contemptuous was James Stuart's favorite pastime, and the weekend promised a limitless opportunity to indulge in it.

Lachlan Forsyth counted the campers in the parking area and decided that it was time for him to set up his souvenir stall. He could afford, at most, a two-drink delay. The opening ceremonies were set to begin at 6 P.M., by which time an assortment of the curious, the obnoxious, and the deluded would be packed three-deep around him, demanding tartan ties, Nessie key rings, and directions to the loo. His answer to all of these queries was: "Right over there on the table."

Often people would recognize his burr and want to know where he was from, in which case a glance at their tartan was always helpful. He told the MacDonalds that he was from Kintyre, while the Campbells were led to believe that he hailed from Argyll; no one ever knew the difference.

Occasionally a well-traveled soul would try to chat him up about various places in Scotland, but Lachlan, well-traveled himself, could field questions indefinitely. He could always recommend a pub or a bed-and-breakfast anywhere between Orkney and the Borders. He could, with equal ease, recite Burns, tell instantly which tartan went with which surname, and settle arguments about the minutiae of Scottish history. It was all part of his job as a professional Scot. The least agreeable part of this lucrative business was having to suffer fools gladly; but he always managed with a straight face to find a tartan for an Olaff son (MacDonald of the Isles: Viking intermarriage), dredge up a family ghost for any family at all, and listen sympathetically to one more "direct descendant of Flora MacDonald and Bonnie Prince Charlie."

Lachlan began to dust off his Highland games coffee mugs and straighten his tartan scarfs and ties. The new blue and beige ones should go like hotcakes—the Princess Diana tartan, that was. And the Royal Stewart was always a big seller. Never mind that none of the purchasers had the least right in the world to wear the colors of the royal family. It was pretty, easy to find, and usually cheaper than special-ordering the tartan of a lesser-known clan, so it always did well at Scottish gatherings. Lachlan always laid in a generous supply before the festival, and he had never failed to sell out. Between the ignorant and the deluded "descendants" of the Prince, business was always brisk.

"Excuse me," said a woman at his elbow, "could you tell me what tartan my family should wear? We're kin to Mary, Queen of Scots, on my mother's side."

Lachlan Forsyth smiled. Let the games begin.

CHAPTER THREE

The Western Virginia Scottish Festival was held each year on privately owned Glencoe Mountain, a high-altitude tourist attraction a few miles outside the tiny community of Meadow Creek. For most of the year, Glencoe offered (for a modest admission fee) nature trails, camping facilities, hang-gliding exhibitions, and a habitat zoo; but on Labor

Day weekend, the mountain was packed with kilted visitors, and the overflow was lodged in motels from Blacksburg to Pulaski. The mountain's owner, Margaret Duff Hamilton (of Hamilton textile mills), presided over the event as honorary games chairman, and welcomed all the clan chiefs at a sherry party in her summer home. Out of earshot, in the campground, lesser folk had tailgate picnics to the accompaniment of pipe-band practice.

"We're not staying here, are we?" asked Geoffrey, recoiling from the sound of an untuned bagpipe. "I would have nightmares of moose in labor."

"You'll get used to it," Elizabeth assured him. "We're staying in one of those tourist cabins on the creek. The clan reserves one every year for the Maid of the Cat."

"If you have to clean up after *him,* you will earn the title," said Geoffrey, frowning at Cluny. "What do we do now?"

Elizabeth stopped the car beside a whitewashed cabin with a tartan ribbon tied around a porch railing. "Chattan colors. We're in here," she announced. "Let's take in our suitcases, and then go to the meadow and register. We'll get a schedule of events, then decide."

"Is *he* coming?"

"Cluny?" Elizabeth smiled. "He's the guest of honor!"

The tourist cabin was sparsely furnished but clean, and its pine beds and dressers smelled of lemon oil. Geoffrey wandered over to the picture above the table and began to study it with interest. In it a kilted young man was bending over the hand of a pretty woman in green.

"Out, damned spot! Out, I say!" said Geoffrey cheerfully. "I'd always thought of Lady Macbeth as older somehow."

Elizabeth set down the ice chest beside the small refrigerator. "Let me see that."

"I wonder if it's unlucky to have *Macbeth* pictures in your room? Of course, I just quoted from it, so we're doomed anyhow."

"Except for your theatre superstitions, you are practically illiterate," Elizabeth informed him. "That woman is in an eighteenth-century costume. How could it be from *Macbeth*?"

"David Garrick production, I expect."

"That," said Elizabeth, tapping the painting with her forefinger, "is a print of a Joy painting of Bonnie Prince Charlie bidding farewell to Flora MacDonald."

"Who is . . . ?"

"After Culloden, the British were searching the Highlands for Bonnie Prince Charlie, so he hid out on the Isle of Skye. Flora MacDonald helped him to escape from Scotland by disguising him as her maid and smuggling him across the inlet in a rowboat."

"I suppose that involved putting him in a longer skirt," murmured Geoffrey. "He seems to be back in full kilt for the farewell scene, though. Say, are you *sure* this is supposed to be the prince?"

"Of course I'm sure. Why?"

Geoffrey pressed his tie against the kilted figure in the painting. "Because he's not wearing the Royal Stewart tartan!"

Elizabeth sighed. "Clans have more than one plaid, Geoffrey. There are patterns for dress, for hunting, for— Well, never mind. I don't have time to explain it to you because I have to change into *my* kilt. Which bedroom do you want?"

"Whichever one *he* doesn't sleep in."

"I thought I'd put him in the bathroom."

"Not unless you brought a bedpan."

"All right, I'll keep him in the room with me. He'll be good protection."

"Protection from whom? If you're referring to me, cousin dear, the dust bunnies under the bed are all the protection you need. More than enough."

Elizabeth smiled sweetly. "I know."

The Highland festival was held in a large meadow several hundred feet below the peak of Glencoe Mountain. Already the well-mowed field was ringed with open tents, each bearing the standard of a different clan. Early arrivals were strolling about, visiting the hosts at the various tents and studying clan displays. Others gathered around the wooden dance platforms to watch the costumed dancers practice, or inspected the wares at the souvenir stalls. By far the largest crowd had collected around the refreshment tent, a testimony to the effect of ninety-two degree weather on persons in wool outfits.

"How do you stand it?" asked Geoffrey, fanning himself with his program. "You look like a stewed sheep."

Elizabeth dabbed at her forehead. "Well, perhaps this velvet jacket is a bit much, but since I've got Cluny, I think I ought to be in full dress." She straightened the lace jabot at her throat. "Thank goodness I have an extra blouse. Isn't this a pretty kilt?" She twirled to show off the red and blue plaid of Clan MacPherson.

"That's right," said Geoffrey. "Shake and bake. I'm

going to the refreshment tent. Want anything?"

"Not now. It would only give me more to sweat. I'm going to check in at the Chattan headquarters, and then I'll see if Marge and her dogs have arrived."

"I'll find you." Geoffrey nodded toward the bobcat. "You'll be easy to spot."

Elizabeth started off in the direction of the clan displays. Cluny, who was by now used to Highland festivals, put up only a token resistance when his leash was tugged. He could behave perfectly if he chose to, but he always made it clear that his cooperation could not be taken for granted. His yellow eyes flickered around the meadow, sighting nothing of interest, just the black-and-white shapes of noisy primates which matched the sweaty man-smells he'd been getting all afternoon. Cluny yawned.

"Isn't this exciting, kitty?" Elizabeth was saying. "All these beautiful colors! Let's go to the Chattan booth and see who's on duty now."

The first tent on Clan Row belonged to the Campbells. They were flying the family standard: a boar's head emblazoned with the motto *Ne Obliviscaris* (Forget Not), and a cardboard poster on an easel listed the family names associated with Clan Campbell. A woman in a white sundress was straightening a stack of brochures while several other people sat in lawn chairs under the canopy watching the milling tourists. Elizabeth, who felt that being Maid of the Cat obliged her to be friendly to all festival participants, waved and smiled.

The woman with the brochures smiled back, but a voice from the tent called out, "Just a minute, young woman!"

Elizabeth flinched. She recognized the voice.

A gnome of a man in a green and white kilt marched out from the shade of the tent, squinting and scowling.

"Would you like to pet the kitty?" asked Elizabeth innocently.

"I would not," snapped the old man. "I suppose you're the Chattan's Maid of the Cat this year?" Elizabeth nodded. "It's a lot of damned foolishness. Not traditional at all. But if you're bound to do it, I think you ought to observe the Highland customs."

"Oh, really?"

"Women . . . do . . . not . . . wear . . . *kilts!*" He seemed to be strangling with rage.

Elizabeth's eyes narrowed. "And MacPhersons do not take orders from Campbells!"

"At least we don't permit our womenfolk to go around pretending to be men," snapped Dr. Campbell, who was enjoying himself hugely.

"This isn't Scotland; it's America. And a lot of people here would say that *you* were in drag!" Elizabeth jerked Cluny's leash and stalked off.

Colin Campbell's face turned Stewart-of-Appin red. "Young woman, do you know who I am?" he thundered after her.

Elizabeth looked back over her shoulder. "Yes," she said. "I recognized you from your picture on the banner."

It was a good exit line, Elizabeth thought as she swept off in the direction of the Chattan tent, but she felt guilty about having used it. Mother would kill me, she thought. She had just been—never mind the provocation—openly rude to an elderly gentleman, something that well-brought-up young ladies did not do. But, she told herself with a giggle, Geoffrey will love it!

Even so, she decided to be more diplomatic henceforth. She was Maid of the Cat, after all, and she saw that role as a variation of the beauty-queen-on-the-float function: be pretty if you can but be charming if it kills you.

Having resolved to be an ambassador of goodwill, Elizabeth smiled encouragingly at an adorable little boy at the Stewart tent. Little blond boys were so cute, she thought. This one looked about ten years old and he was wearing jeans; she thought he'd look wonderful in a kilt.

"Hello, there!" She beamed at him. "This is Cluny, the Chattan bobcat. Would you like to pet him?"

The boy stared at her, his face a cherubic blank. "No."

"Oh, it's all right! He's had his claws removed, and he doesn't bite. He won't hurt you."

"So?"

Here's a chance to be charming against overwhelming odds, thought Elizabeth. She tried another smile. "Do you have any questions?"

"Just one," said James Stuart McGowan. "If you gain another five pounds, will you have to buy a new kilt, or can they let out this one?"

Elizabeth's smile froze into a grimace. "Are you a Campbell, little boy?" she growled between clenched teeth.

James Stuart shrugged. "I doubt it."

"Well, you ought to be!"

By the time she arrived at the Clan Chattan tent, Elizabeth was feeling more like the Queen of Hearts than the queen of the Rose Bowl. Off with their heads! She had now been rude to old people and children; she felt like a boiled owl in her wool outfit; and so far she had not seen anyone she knew. "Not one of my better days," said Elizabeth to Cluny. He was washing his paw and did not bother to look up.

"We're here!" she called out with as much cheerfulness as she could muster.

A plump woman in white shorts got up from a lawn chair. Pinned to the shoulder of her white blouse was a scarf of the MacPherson tartan. "Oh, dear," she murmured. "I'm not sure what to do with the mascot. Betty is in charge, and she isn't here yet. They had an out-of-town guest, I think . . ."

Elizabeth sighed. "I'll settle for a drink. Cluny probably needs one, too. Do you have an ice chest? We can drain off the water into a cup for him."

The woman edged away from them. "He won't bite, will he?"

"If he doesn't get some water, he might. Where are the cups?"

Elizabeth scooped out some ice water for the bobcat while the substitute hostess straightened pamphlets and murmured, "I'm sure Betty will be here soon." The occupants of the other lawn chairs were discussing home computers.

"Do you want Cluny to stay here? I wanted to go over and see the border collies, but I'm afraid he might scare them."

The woman didn't know, she was sure.

Elizabeth sat down in the grass and began to stroke Cluny's brindled fur. "I wonder what Geoffrey's doing," she mused.

James Stuart McGowan had managed to give his parents

the slip, and he was wandering around the meadow looking for something to do. The only other children he'd seen so far were toddlers; he certainly didn't want to be bothered with them. He was briefly tempted by the refreshment tent, but that would be the first place his parents would look for him—better avoid it for a while. If he knew Babs, he had about another hour before she lost it completely and had him paged over the loudspeaker system.

He edged his way past the dancing platforms with an ill-concealed sneer and wandered over to a souvenir booth. The old man behind the counter looked like the wizard in *Star Wars*. That qualified him as mildly interesting, James Stuart thought. Behind the white ruff of beard lay a pleasant expression and a pair of sharp blue eyes that twinkled all the same. James Stuart didn't think the man looked grandfatherly: *his* grandfather lived in a chrome-and-glass apartment and went to a tanning salon. The lack of resemblance was in the stranger's favor, but he had his doubts about the wardrobe. The man wore a tartan tam, a lace-up shirt with white puffed sleeves, and the full regalia of a kilt. The only other person nearby was a young guy in yellow slacks who was flipping through the tie racks.

James Stuart noticed the fancy daggers in the display case, and decided that this was as good a place as any to waste a couple of minutes. He leaned forward to examine the jewel on the dagger's hilt. The costumed proprietor turned away from the tie racks with a regulation smile and bore down upon the new customer.

"Hoots man, and what would a wee bairn like yoursel' be wantin' wi' a dirk o' that ilk? And where might ye be from, laddie?"

James Stuart looked him up and down with his most withering stare. "Earth," he said at last.

Geoffrey looked up from his perusal of a Campbell necktie and laughed. "Pretty clever, kid!" he said admiringly. "I'll buy you a drink on the strength of that. Want a root beer?"

The icy gaze transferred itself to Geoffrey. "No, mister. And I don't want to ride in your car either." James Stuart felt a glimmer of satisfaction as he watched the red-faced young man stalk off in the direction of the refreshment tent. "How much is the dagger?" he asked.

"Depends, lad," said the proprietor with a considerably diminished accent. "Will you be taking it or wearing it between your shoulder blades?"

James Stuart smiled. This grown-up knew his way around. "What do you call these knives?"

"*Skian dubh.* That translates to black knife. Natural stag horn with sterling silver fittings, that one is. The Highlanders used to wear them in their socks. Not fancy ones like these, though. I reckon they cut their onions with it."

"It's real, isn't it?"

"That it is, Jimmy."

James Stuart looked up sharply. "How did you know my name?"

The old man smiled. "Why, didn't ye know that Celtic people have The Sight?" he asked. "You know—what you call the ESP."

James Stuart nodded. "What's your name?"

The old man inclined his head. "Lachlan Forsyth at your service. Want to tell me the rest of yours?" He added hastily, "I don't like to overstrain mah powers, you know."

34

"James Stuart McGowan. At school they call me Jimmy."

"McGowan, eh?" Lachlan Forsyth nodded. "I take it you're a hostage?"

"What?"

"Dragged here by your parents, man. Given 'em the slip, have you?"

James Stuart smirked. "They never find me unless I want them to."

"Don't be too sure of that, lad." Over the boy's shoulder, Lachlan could see two interesting figures: one anxious blond woman approaching the stall at full speed and one diffident young man in a Buchanan tartan who kept signaling for Lachlan to come and talk to him. The old man gave him a slight nod, and turned back to the matter at hand. "Might that be your mother coming now?"

James Stuart turned around just as his mother reached the stall. "Hello," he said coolly. "Put my picture on any milk cartons yet?"

His mother decided to ignore him, in favor of the third party present. "I'm really sorry if he's been bothering you," she told Lachlan. "I only turned my back for an instant."

"Nae bother," said Lachlan with his most practiced smile. "Are you needing him for something?"

"Why . . . er . . . no. In fact, his father and I have been invited to a little get-together, and we weren't sure—"

"See? You're not able to have any fun yourselves, being burdened with the baby-sitting chores, whereas I'm stuck here in this wee stall in dire need of a capable young assistant like Jimmy here."

Babs McGowan blinked. She was so used to apologizing for her son that it took her a moment to frame an alternate reply.

"In fact," Lachlan went on smoothly, "the lad and I were just coming to an agreement about this lovely *skian dubh,* a relic of your very own clan, madam. We had just decided that he could help me out selling the goods here for a commission of five per cent, which he could use to buy the dagger. It would be ever so much of a help for an old man like myself to be able to take a wee break now and again."

"How about ten per cent?" countered James Stuart.

"Can't spare the profit margin, lad," said Lachlan, still twinkling. "But a'course, if you'd rather spend the holiday with your mum and dad, there'll be no hard feelings from here." He took the dagger out of the jewelry case and began to polish its metal sheath with a tartan scarf.

"It looks a little dangerous," said Babs McGowan doubtfully.

"Five percent, then!" cried James Stuart. "I'll start now."

"I'm not sure . . ."

Lachlan waved her away. "You've a party to get to, haven't you? Leave the lad to me. As another of your clansmen put it: 'You deserve a break today.' Right, Jimmy? We'll see you in a wee while, madam."

Babs McGowan wandered away, wondering how long it would be before she was paged and implored to return for her son.

"Now then," said Lachlan Forsyth when she was out of earshot, "I'll just give you a bit of an intro to the goods here, right? Now, most of the prices are marked on the items. See, here on this key chain, there's a four-dash. That means four dollars. Your biggest problem will be the folks who come up wanting clan items without a clue as to which one they belong to. They don't belong to any, like as not. But look here: this little book lists all the surnames associated with Scottish clans. So you get the bloke to tell you his last name, and you look it up, right?"

James Stuart frowned. "Suppose the name isn't in here?"

"Well, you ask for other family names. Their mum's maiden name, or their granny's. Sooner or later you're bound to hit one that turns up in the book, and then you sing it out and find the tartan for whatever clan it is."

"But I don't know tartans."

"I wouldn't expect you to, lad. They're all marked on the back with little silver stickers. And see this one? That's the Caledonia tartan, which belongs to no family at all. It's just general Scots plaid, for anybody. So if you can't match up a name with a clan, you just give them this one and they'll be happy."

James Stuart began to leaf through the clan book. "Harper . . . *Buchanan;* Hathorn . . . *MacDonald* . . . Miller . . . *MacFarlane.* Got it."

"Dead easy, isn't it?"

"I guess so. But aren't you fooling them with that Caledonia one?"

"Aren't you the trusting one, though? I'll tell you, Jimmy, seeing as how we're in business together now: it's no more of a sham than the rest of 'em."

"It isn't? Why?"

"Because clan ties aren't as easy as coming up with the right last name, of course, but people don't want to know that. Here, I'll give you an example. This one, Miller—

Clan Buchanan it says, right? Well, you've only got to think about last names to see how daft that is. Because the great majority of surnames came in one of two ways, lad: occupation or patronym."

"What was that last one?"

"Patronym. The first name of your dad. So you might be John's son—Johnson; or Robert's son—Robertson; or Andrew's son—Anderson. You see the way of it?" James Stuart nodded. "But all the Johnsons aren't related, are they? Cause why?"

James Stuart smirked. "Because they were probably descended from a thousand different Johns."

"Right you are, lad. And it gets even stickier than that. Here, what's your dad's first name?"

"Stuart."

"And what about *his* dad?"

"Um . . . Arthur. Why?"

"Because last names didn't stay the same in the old days, not when people took their fathers' names. See, your dad would be Stuart MacArthur—son of Arthur—but you'd be Jimmy MacStuart, because you're the son of Stuart. Now, all that changed around the sixteenth century, most likely when the bureaucrats decided to get things organized. So they say to you: we can't be having all this surname-changing 'cause we don't know who's who; so from now on your lot will be MacStuarts, and it won't change. But you see—if they'd put a stop to the name-changing twenty years earlier, in your grandad's time, your family would be MacArthurs instead. Do you see? So a Johnson might just as easily have been a MacDonald or a Robertson. It was the luck of his dad's name when the changing stopped, and it doesn't prove a pennyworth of kinship with anybody else."

"What does MacGowan come from?"

"Oh, well, that takes us back to occupations, lad. In Gaelic, a *gow* was a blacksmith. So you can be fairly certain that one of your ancestors could shoe a horse, but how do you know whether he was the smith of Kintyre or the smith of Dundee, or one of the other few hundred living all over Scotland?"

James Stuart thought it over. "Was it the same with Millers?"

"There was a mill in every town, lad. And there were Coopers making barrels, and Fletchers making arrows, and Weavers spinning cloth—but there's no saying that the Weaver in a given clan was the one you got your name from, is there?"

"How could you be sure?"

Lachlan Forsyth stopped dusting the thistle-patterned china and shook his head. "Call it equal quantities of luck and hard work, Jimmy. You check shipping records to trace your ancestor back to Scotland—that's if you know what port and what date he came in. And you check out his birth records in Scotland—that's if you can trace him back to his place of origin. And you hope the courthouse or the parish church didn't burn within the past few centuries. Believe me, it's a lot easier to call out a last name and have someone look in a book and assign you a clan. It means about as much in the end."

James Stuart thought about the large enameled plaque in the McGowan den, which bore the arms of Clan MacPherson. "Why doesn't it make any difference?" he asked.

"Ask me again," said Lachlan, noticing that the man in the Buchanan tartan was about to walk away. "I'm in need of a break. You ought to be able to hold down the fort for a quarter of an hour. Change is in the tin box there. One last thing. Tartan ties are eight dollars, and scarves are ten. Got it?"

James Stuart nodded. "Ties eight; scarves ten."

"Right. Do your best, lad. Remember your five per cent." He hurried away from the stall with a beaming smile to an approaching customer. "My assistant will be happy to help you, mum!" he called back.

The woman fingered the rack of plaids. "I'm a Logan, and I'd like to get a tartan for my husband. How much are they?"

James Stuart gave his best imitation of his mentor's feral smile. "Yes, ma'am. Logan. The ties are ten dollars, and the scarves are twelve. Cash."

CHAPTER FOUR

Cluny, sprawled on the warm grass in feline oblivion, looked considerably more comfortable than Elizabeth felt. She was holding her third cup of ice water—trying to decide whether to drink it or pour it over her head—when Betty Carson appeared with a stranger in tow.

"Elizabeth! Wonderful to see you!" She gave Elizabeth the hug that Southern women substitute for a cordial nod. "I know everyone must be frantic because I'm so late."

"They've managed to bear up," said Elizabeth, glancing at the lawn-chair contingent. They were still discussing home computers without visible signs of distress.

Betty Carson's steel-ribbed smile took in the idyllic scene and the half-empty bottle of Johnnie Walker. "Leave them to me," she said briskly. "I'll get this bunch working. Oh, Elizabeth! This is Cameron Dawson, a new professor in Andy's department, and you'll never guess where he's from!" The young man looked so embarrassed by this that Elizabeth decided not to try. When no answer was forthcoming, Betty said triumphantly, "Edinburgh! Isn't it grand? He's practically right off the plane. Anyway, I have a blue million things to do, so I'm leaving him in your charge. Cameron, you'll be in good hands. She's Maid of the Cat for your clan. I'll find you later!"

Cameron watched his hostess march off toward the Chattan tent, with the sinking feeling of one who has been abandoned in the asylum. His new keeper was a frazzled young woman in what appeared to be a wool outfit, with a lynx on a chain lead. He wondered if she represented anybody famous; Morgan Le Fay came to mind, but it might be uncivil to ask. He thought she might be very pretty in a less ludicrous climate. What must the temperature be on this mountain? They'd measure it in Kelvin degrees, he was certain of that. Cameron dabbed at his forehead and endeavored to look pleasant.

"Hello," said the young woman. "My name is Elizabeth. I guess you can tell my last name," she added, pointing to her skirt.

What can she mean? thought Cameron. A last name from a skirt . . . Weaver? Taylor? Dirndl?

"I don't understand," he admitted.

"Didn't you recognize the MacPherson tartan?"

"No, I'm afraid not. I don't know much about that sort

of thing."

"I thought Betty said you were Clan MacPherson."

"So she tells me," sighed Cameron. "Actually, I'm a marine biologist, and I'm much more familiar with porpoises and seals than with history."

"Seals! Oh, the Selkies! Banished to the sea for being neutral in the battle of good and evil. *I am a man upon the land, I am a Selkie o-oon tha sea!*" She hummed a bit of the tune. Elizabeth had finished her folk-medicine course and enrolled in Folklore 5270.

Cameron stared. He knew that there was an odd religious sect somewhere in Virginia; his hosts had mentioned it in passing. Perhaps she was a member. At any rate, she seemed to believe in animal transmutation. He nodded toward the bobcat. "What about him?"

"Cluny? He's a bobcat. I'm Maid of the Cat."

"Ah. He's your father then?"

"Who?"

"The lynx."

Elizabeth shook her head. "Are you sure you're a biologist?"

"Practically the only thing I'm certain of just now. Why?"

"Because, if you think people are descended from bobcats, you'll be a novelty at the university."

"Oh, that. I was humoring *you*. Selkies, indeed!"

Elizabeth smiled. "Folklore," she said. "I'm doing graduate work in anthropology. Would you like me to show you around?"

"Might as well. I suppose I should see what these things are like."

"I guess the ones in Scotland are much larger," said Elizabeth.

"Don't know. Never went to one."

She glanced at his shorts and Save-the-Whales T-shirt. "And I suppose you thought it was too hot to wear your kilt today?"

"Haven't got one."

Elizabeth took a deep breath. "Look," she said, "do you speak Gaelic? Do you play a bagpipe? Do you read Walter Scott? Do you believe in the Loch Ness monster?"

"None of the above. Sorry."

She grinned. "Well, come along. I'll be your guide. God knows you're going to need one."

Lachlan Forsyth and his orange-kilted companion had stopped to watch the dancers practice, careful to be just out of earshot of the other spectators. Lachlan, nodding in time to the tape-recorded bagpipe music, seemed unaware of the other's nervousness. "Lovely tune that," he remarked. "It's a doddle to dance to."

Jerry Buchanan glanced nervously about. "Can we talk here?" he whispered.

"Aye, laddie, and we'd be that much safer if you would'na look sa guilty."

"I'm sorry. I don't want to jeopardize the Cause."

"I know," said Lachlan kindly.

"It's going all right, isn't it? I haven't read anything about it in the newspapers."

"I know."

"Is that good?"

"Aye."

"Have you been in touch with . . ." Jerry couldn't think of any discreet way to phrase it. "With anybody?" he finished lamely.

"Aye. The secret is safe, but the progress is slow. It's a matter of money. We'd get donations if we advertised, but we have to be particular about who we tell."

"Is there going to be any kind of a sign here at the games? Some way that I can tell who's with the Cause."

"Aye, laddie. But if I tell you, you must swear not to discuss it with a soul. I would ken an enemy, but you couldna'. Do ya swear tae silence?"

Jerry nodded vigorously. "Oh, of course, Mr. Forsyth! *Absolutely.*"

"Well, since you're a Buchanan . . ."

"I wish I weren't," sighed Jerry, glancing at his rainbow kilt.

"There's worse things, laddie. There were Buchanans at Agincourt and Flodden, mind ye remember. But you asked for a sign. Will you be going to the Hill-Sing tonight?"

Jerry tried to remember when that cocktail party was being held in the Hutchesons' camper. Had he promised to be there, or just said that he might drop by? It didn't matter—not compared to this. "Of course I'll be there if you want me to," he said.

"Right. Good lad. Now, at the singing, when they begin 'Flower of Scotland,' you stand up. And look around to see who else is standing up, and there's your sign."

" 'Flower of Scotland'? It's a folk song?"

The old man gave him a solemn stare. "It's the national anthem of the Republic of Scotland."

Jerry Buchanan gasped. "About donations," he whispered. "Would another thousand help?"

Lachlan Forsyth smiled. "Aye."

"That," said Elizabeth, "is a bagpipe."

"Oh, good!" cried Cameron. "Let's borrow it and vacuum the cat!"

After an ominous pause, Elizabeth began to laugh. "*Monty Python*, I presume?"

"*The Goon Show*, I think."

"I take it you don't listen to this much at home?"

"I'm very fond of Scottish music. Sheena Easton, Rod Stewart. . . . The porpoises love Rod Stewart." His face brightened as it always did when he could get the subject around to marine biology. Elizabeth looked at him in his Save-the-Whales T-shirt, and beyond him at the kilted Americans playing bagpipes. He's like a time traveler, she thought. But if he is *now,* then what time are we?

Aloud she said, "I'll bet you'd like to see the refreshment tent. They have any amount of weird food there that you're not going to find in the Shop-Rite near the university."

"What, haggis with neeps and tatties followed by a clootie dumpling?"

Elizabeth frowned. "Clootie means the devil, doesn't it?"

"Not on a menu. It's a cloth-wrapped dumpling. What's *that?*"

She turned to look at a blue-kilted man wearing a khaki shirt and an Australian bush hat. "A Douglas, I think."

"Kangaroo branch. He ought to have a wallaby in his sporran. Are we headed for the refreshment stand?"

"Keep going. It's at the end of this row of tents, but if you keep turning around like that, it'll take us two hours to get there."

Cameron, who was staring at passersby, didn't seem to have heard. "A *cowboy* hat? What's that—the Highland cowboy?" Suddenly he noticed the tent of a regional Scottish society. "Piedmont Highlanders. *Piedmont* Highlanders? Isn't that a contradiction in terms?"

Their progress was slowed further. Having noticed the signs on each tent, Cameron began to use them as an exercise in free association. "Grant—that's a furniture store in Glasgow . . . Menzies—John Menzies; I buy my books there . . . Barclay—the banking folks . . . and Gordon's gin, of course."

Elizabeth shook her head. "You're going to be crushed when the MacDonald tent doesn't have golden arches, aren't you?"

Cameron wasn't listening. "What is that great horde of people doing there?"

"That's the refreshment tent." Elizabeth sighed. "Pick a line."

They edged their way past a collection of pipe-band members, and peered over the crowd to see what the menu offered.

"Bridies!" cried Cameron. "Mutton pies!"

What does one talk about to marine biologists, wondered Elizabeth, especially if one doesn't know much about seals or porpoises. And a Scottish marine biologist, at that. Something clicked. "Loch Ness!" she cried.

"That's up near Inverness. I went camping there with the Scouts once, though."

"I don't get it. I mention Loch Ness, and you think of Boy Scouts. As a marine biologist, shouldn't you be interested in Nessie?"

"An unverified creature in a freshwater lake? Why should I?"

"I don't know, but I'll bet you're going to be asked about Nessie an awful lot while you're over here."

"Well, it'll make a change from folks wanting to know if I'm Irish or asking what it's like in Edin*burg*." He shuddered. "And that was only in the bloody airport."

"Well, you should feel better here," said Elizabeth. "These folks know all about Scotland. There'll probably be people here who vacationed in Inverness—"

"Inver*ness*," Cameron corrected her.

"Or Aberdeen—"

"Aber*deen*."

"And one of the Menzies is really a war buff. He'll probably want to talk to you about . . ." Elizabeth took a deep breath and marshaled her linguistic forces. "Ban*noch*burrn!" She finished triumphantly.

"You don't have to go through all that," said Cameron mildly. "It's *Ban*nockburn. A bannock is an oatmeal cake. Speaking of food, here we are at the counter. I'll have a mutton pie and a sausage roll, please. Do y'have any Irn Bru?"

"Strictly non-alcoholic here," whispered Elizabeth.

He laughed. "It's a carbonated drink. Comes in a can."

"Oh."

"Would you like to get anything for your moggie?" Seeing her look of bewilderment, he pointed to Cluny. "For your dad there."

"No, he's already eaten." Elizabeth smiled. "We could take this stuff up on the hill, if you like. From under the

47

trees, we'll be able to see the games."

"Will they be throwing the hammer this way?"

"We won't sit behind the Campbell tent. Come on."

When they had settled under an oak tree, with sausage rolls balanced on their laps, Elizabeth said, "Are you over here to work on anything specific?"

It was an inspired question. Cameron launched into an animated explanation of seal migratory patterns, which might have been quite educational if Elizabeth had listened. She sat nibbling her pastry, and nodding occasionally with an expression of rapt interest. Cameron began to talk about manatees in the South Atlantic. Elizabeth hung on every syllable, listening to the vowel sounds, the trilled *r*'s and uvular *l*'s, and making no sense at all of the words.

Brown eyes, she was thinking. I thought Scots had blue eyes. And his hair is so pretty. What would you call that color? Russet? Sorrel?

". . . which has interesting evolutionary implications, don't you agree?"

Elizabeth sighed. "I love your *r*'s."

Cameron blinked. "Er—ah—yours is quite nice, too."

"No, I can't make them sound at all the way you do. Ag-*rree*."

"Oh! *r*'s. I thought—never mind. Anyway, about the sound patterns—"

"Yes, they're wonderful," she murmured.

"You've heard whale songs, then?"

Elizabeth straightened up. "Whales? I was talking about *your* sound patterns."

Cameron blushed. "That shouldn't be a novelty here. What percentage of these people are from Scotland?"

"Just you, I imagine," Elizabeth told him. "When the rest of us say we're Scottish, we mean six generations back."

"Hmmm." Cameron studied the faces of the passersby. "Now *that's* a Scottish face," he announced. "Look at that old man in the souvenir stall. I'll bet he's the real thing."

"I don't know. Maybe."

"Come on. Let's go and find out. Maybe he has some Billy Connolly tapes."

"Who's Billy Connolly?"

Cameron considered it. Whom could you compare Billy Connolly to? Richard Pryor? Lenny Bruce? He grinned. "He's the Duke of Glasgow. Come on."

Lachlan Forsyth, having finished his conference with Jerry Buchanan, returned to the stall to find Jimmy in conference with a man in full MacDonald regalia.

"How are you keeping, lad?" he asked pleasantly.

Jimmy froze, thinking for an instant that Lachlan's ESP had told him about the extra twenty per cent he'd been pocketing; but he decided that it might just be a Scottish way of saying hello, so he answered carefully, "Just fine, sir. But this guy has a special request, and I don't know what to do about him."

"Och aye?" said Lachlan, turning his performance on the customer. "How can I help, Mr. . . . MacDonald, wouldn't it be?"

"Hutcheson, actually." The man shook Lachlan's hand. "Dr. Walter Hutcheson. I was looking for a tartan for my wife."

"Well, we have the MacDonald hunting, which is a nice green, or perhaps a dress plaid in the ancient colors?"

"No. I don't need MacDonald. You see, my wife is from Scotland. She's the niece of the Duke of Rothesay, and I'd like to find out what tartan she'd take and get her a scarf in it. I don't know much about these things myself."

Lachlan Forsyth looked thoughtful. "The Duke of Rothesay, eh? I'd like very much to meet her."

Dr. Hutcheson smiled. "Heather's back at the camper now. I'll try to bring her by sometime, though. Do you have her plaid in stock?"

The old man produced a fringed scarf patterned in soft blues and beige. "Her ladyship would be entitled to wear this one," he declared. "No one more so."

"Oh, Heather doesn't bother with all that title business," said her husband with a touch of pride. "She hates for me to tell people about it. Now that she's in America, she says she wants to be plain old Mrs. Hutcheson. I'll bring her by."

"Right. Do that. Oh, look—here comes the MacPhersons' Maid of the Cat. Wonder what she's about. Here, doctor, my assistant can take care of the purchase for you. He needs the practice." Lachlan waved to the couple approaching the stall. "Hello, Moggie!" he called to the bobcat. "Who are your friends here?"

"Hi!" said Elizabeth. "Do you have any tapes by the Duke of Glasgow?"

Lachlan Forsyth looked puzzled. "Dukes again! Tapes, d'ye say? By the Duke of Glasgow?"

Behind Elizabeth, Cameron mouthed, "Bil-ly Con-nol-ly."

Lachlan grinned. "Oh, aye! Is it him you're wanting? Lassie, I'm truly sorry. Not many Americans appreciate

His Grace, so I don't carry his work. You come to see me at the Grandfather games next July, and I'll see what I can do for you." He turned to Cameron. "You should've brought some with you, laddie. Where are you from? Kelvinside, from the look of you."

"Edinburgh," said Cameron.

"Ah, Morningside, then. Just over, are you?"

Lachlan and Cameron began to talk animatedly about the Rangers. Elizabeth, deciding that she wasn't interested in British military matters, began to look at the stall displays when she noticed the man at her side.

"Dr. Hutcheson!" she cried. "I'm so glad to see you. It's been ages! I'm Elizabeth MacPherson, remember?"

"Ah, yes! The little girl who used to be so crazy about border collies. I see you're still fond of livestock." He nodded toward Cluny.

"Yes. He's the Chattan mascot. I'll leave him with my cousin when I go to see the collies. Is Marge out with them or back at the camper?"

Dr. Hutcheson reddened. "I guess most people here haven't heard. Marge and I are no longer married." Seeing Elizabeth's look of astonishment, he hurried on. "We—ah—came to a parting of the ways about a year ago, and I've remarried. Is that your husband?" he asked, glancing at Cameron.

"No," murmured Elizabeth. "He's a professor from Scotland. I'm showing him around."

"Scotland! Well, isn't that something? Heather's from Scotland too! Why don't you bring him by the camper this evening for our get-together?"

"I'll ask Cameron." She wasn't thinking clearly enough

51

to come up with a glib excuse not to go. The news about the divorce had caught her off guard. Still, maybe Cameron would enjoy meeting another Scot. She should ask him, at least.

"You won't have any trouble finding us in the campground," Dr. Hutcheson was saying. "We're flying the MacDonald banner, since I'm regional clan president. Of course, Heather isn't a MacDonald by birth." He pulled out a corner of the newly purchased scarf. "That's *her* tartan." He reeled off Heather's pedigree as if she were a sheepdog. "But don't mention to her that I told you. You know how people are about the aristocracy."

"I think so," said Elizabeth, giving him a meaningful stare. "Is Marge here on her own, do you think?"

Dr. Hutcheson's lips tightened. "I haven't seen her. Do stop by later, both of you." He nodded curtly and walked away.

Cameron looked up from his discussion with Lachlan in time to hear the last few words. "Stop by?" he echoed.

"He's the local chief of the MacDonalds," Elizabeth explained. "And his new wife is Scottish, so he wants us to come by later and meet her."

Cameron, detecting a note of bitterness in Elizabeth's voice, said, "I don't mind. Do you want to?"

"Maybe. I have to find somebody first. Can I meet you later? At the Chattan tent around seven?"

"Leave him with me!" boomed Lachlan. "I'm having a high time hearing about the Rangers bashing the Celtics."

Elizabeth's eyes flashed. "As a Gaelic people, I should think you'd be more sympathetic to the troubles in Northern Ireland!" Without waiting for an answer, she swept away.

Lachlan and Cameron exchanged puzzled glances. What did Belfast have to do with Scottish soccer matches?

CHAPTER FIVE

Elizabeth found Geoffrey at the sign-up booth for athletic events. "What on earth are you doing?" she demanded.

He shrugged. "Well, I thought I'd get into the spirit of things. Learn how to do something. It might be useful for *Brigadoon.* What have you been up to?"

Elizabeth smiled. "Can you do without me for a while? I've met somebody . . ."

Geoffrey raised his eyebrows. "Oh? What's he like?"

"Mmmm. He looks like Prince Philip did when he married Queen Elizabeth."

"Oh! He's Greek!"

Elizabeth scowled. "He's from Scotland. He has a Ph.D. in marine biology, and the way he talks is just lethally sexy."

"Oh. Scottish. Too bad."

"What do you mean, too bad?"

Geoffrey grinned. "Remember what you told me earlier? All the Highland clansmen were either murdered after Culloden or driven out of Scotland. So if this guy comes from there . . ."

"Shut up, Geoffrey. You always exaggerate. Anyway, I don't care if there were sharks in his gene pool, he's adorable. And he has an accent like pancake syrup—all *l*'s and *r*'s." She sighed.

Geoffrey groaned. "Are you going to get a grip on yourself, or do I have to turn the hose on you?"

Elizabeth made a face at him.

"And what about your boyfriend the grave robber?"

"Milo?" She hesitated. "Well . . . we aren't engaged or anything. I told Mary Gillespie we were, but that was in self-defense. Anyway, I'm just showing Cameron around the games."

"From the way you were talking earlier, it sounds as if he'll need a bodyguard to protect him from his guide."

"Oh, you're worse than Bill. Anyway, what are you doing right now?"

"Why do you ask, cousin?"

"Because I want to go to the dog field, and I need you to keep the moggie for me."

"The . . . *moggie?*" echoed Geoffrey in forbidding tones.

"Bobcat, Geoffrey. Anyway, can you keep him for an hour, please? You're not scheduled for any games now, are you?"

"Not till tomorrow. I signed up for something called a saber toss. The idiot that typed the sheet misspelled it, though."

Elizabeth smiled. "It should be very interesting. I wouldn't miss it for the world. See you later!"

Andy Carson found his visiting Scottish professor at Lachlan Forsyth's souvenir stall, discussing gardening— something about a Partick thistle. "Here you are!" he exclaimed, clapping Cameron on the shoulder. "What do you think of the games so far, eh?"

"It's a bit like Disneyland," murmured Cameron.

"Just like home, eh!" boomed Andy, who never listened to other people's small talk. "Well, come over here. I'd like you to meet a clan chief."

Cameron shook hands with the wizened man in a green kilt. "How do you do, sir?"

Andy Carson performed the introductions. "Dr. Campbell here is an M.D., Cameron, but he's also a member of the board of trustees at the university."

"Class of '39," grunted Dr. Campbell.

"He's been one of our chief supporters for the Center of Marine Science." Turning to Colin Campbell, Andy explained, "Dr. Dawson here is our visiting marine biologist from Scotland."

"Excellent," said Dr. Campbell with a thrust of his jaw. "About time you people got an expert in here. Though you Scots haven't done such a good job over there."

"At Great Cumbrae? Our work on seal migration—"

"Seals? Who gives a good goddamn about seals, young man? What have you done about Nessie?" Without waiting for an answer, he edged in closer. "There's been another sighting here, you know."

Cameron blinked. First selkies, then bobcats, and now sea serpents. He wondered if jet lag ever caused people to hallucinate. He hoped so. America couldn't *really* be like this . . . could it?

"I work with seals and porpoises," he said faintly.

Dr. Campbell wasn't listening. "It was in the Eastern Bay this time. That's an arm of the Chesapeake right across from Annapolis, Maryland. Scared the hell out of a couple in a sailboat. You people are familiar with Chessie, aren't you? Have you seen the 1982 videotape? How does it compare with Nessie?"

"I don't know," said Cameron. "Maybe a paleontologist

could advise you—"

"Well, consult one," snapped Colin Campbell. "The Center can afford it. I've certainly donated enough money to it."

"I haven't had much time to talk to Dr. Dawson, Colin," Andy Carson put in hurriedly. "He hasn't even visited the Center yet. Maybe we should postpone this little talk until—"

"What *do* you know about Nessie, young man?" Dr. Campbell barked.

"F.—all," said Cameron. "Which is all I want to know."

Andy Carson laughed nervously. "That dry British sense of humor, eh, Dawson? I'm sure you don't realize how important Dr. Campbell is to our department. Why, his efforts on the board of trustees were instrumental in getting this center set up in the first place. His donations played a big part in endowing the visiting professorship you received."

"Are you saying that you took me away from North Sea seal studies to come over here and study sea serpents?" cried Cameron. "A year's work down the bloody cludgie!"

"Get somebody else, Carson!" snapped Colin Campbell.

"Now, gentlemen, please. This is a social event—"

"Right," said Cameron. "I have no intention of discussing it further until we do so officially. Excuse me, please." Without waiting for an answer, he walked away. A dozen yards from Lachlan's stall, he stopped and looked about. Kilted people edged past him on either side, but he didn't see anyone he knew. At least it wasn't so hot anymore.

Cameron glanced up at the sky. So that was it! A bloody great cloud had settled over the meadow. He felt a drop of rain hit his cheek. Some outing this had turned out to be. He was trying to decide whether to seek shelter when he caught sight of something familiar. Cluny the bobcat was rubbing up against a tent pole, while beside him a crowd of people were huddled together, perilously close to treading on him. Cameron hurried over.

"Hello!" he called out. "Elizabeth! Are you here?" The bobcat's lead unwound from the throng of people, but the person at the other end of it was not the Maid of the Cat. A young man in yellow poplin slacks looked at him inquiringly.

"Sorry," stammered Cameron. "I was looking for a dark-haired young lady who had charge of the lynx earlier."

Geoffrey pointed an accusing finger at Cameron. "Pancake syrup!" he cried.

"Oh God!" thought Cameron. "Maybe it's something in their water supply. Has anyone ever checked America's water supply for mind-altering substances?"

Geoffrey smiled. "I've heard of you," he explained. "The young lady you're looking for is my cousin Elizabeth. She left this beast with me while she went to look at sheepdogs. Would you like to watch him for her?" This last hopeful query was nearly drowned out by a clap of thunder.

Cameron hesitated. "Do you know which way she went?"

"In that direction," said Geoffrey, pointing. "Come on, I'll see if we can find her."

The rain was pelting down even harder now, punctuated by flashes of lightning, all of which made Cluny even less anxious than usual to walk on his leash—particularly when foolish people were trying to make him head for an open field in a thunderstorm.

"Damned cat!" yelled Geoffrey over the rain. "We'll never get there at this rate!"

"How far is it?" Cameron called back.

They had left the circle of clan tents and were headed for the lower meadow where the herding practice took place. The wind, blowing from that direction, had pretty well drenched them after the first two minutes.

"She won't be out in this downpour!" cried Geoffrey. "I think we ought to wait it out on the hill under the trees. But first I'm going to stash this cat somewhere!"

Beside a stack of boards and some concrete drainpipes, Geoffrey noticed a long wooden box with a latched door. Reasoning that this was probably a cage meant for Cluny in the first place, Geoffrey flipped up the latch and shoved the bobcat in headfirst. A rumble of thunder covered any sounds of feline displeasure at such cavalier treatment, and Geoffrey, the rain dribbling down his neck, closed the door and sped up the hill toward Cameron.

A few moments later they were settled at the base of a relatively dry oak, watching the sports field turn into a mud puddle.

"Do you come to these things often?" asked Cameron politely.

"God, no! It's a boot camp for lunatics." Cameron laughed at that, and Geoffrey added, "That's a line from *Brigadoon*. My community theatre group is doing the play, so I came to soak up atmosphere."

"Is it about Scotland?"

"Don't you know it? It's a Lerner and Loewe musical. Brigadoon is an eighteenth-century Scottish village that doesn't want to be corrupted by progress, so their minister prays for a miracle to keep them from having to change."

"What happens?"

"The village only exists one day out of every century. See, they'd go to bed in 1753, and when they woke up in the morning it would be 1853, and so on. But the village always stays the same. Neat trick, huh?"

Cameron frowned. "Well, it has some drawbacks, you know. One day they will wake up to find themselves in the parking lot of the Aberdeen Hilton, I bet."

"Great idea! I wonder if I could talk Sinclair into doing an epilogue?"

"Have the games given you any inspiration?"

"The costumes are quite good. I may make a few sketches tonight. But what has really been interesting is viewing everything from the context of *Brigadoon*. I mean, this farce practically *is* Brigadoon. The festival exists one day a year; and no matter what's happening in Scotland, it's still Bonnie Prince Charlie-time here on the mountain."

"Spot on!" Cameron nodded. "It certainly isn't the Scotland I come from. But at least they seem to be enjoying themselves. Your cousin, for instance."

"I think the rain is beginning to slack off. Cloud must be moving," said Geoffrey, peering up at the sky. "You're right, of course, about—did she tell you the family's pet name for her, by the way?"

"No."

Geoffrey smiled. "I thought not. When Elizabeth was little, her older brother Bill claimed not to be able to pronounce the name, so he called her something else."

"That's not uncommon. Elizabeth is difficult to say, I should think."

"Yes, but they will never convince me that three-year-old Bill, unable to say *Elizabeth,* should do such a first-rate job of pronouncing *Lizard-Breath.*"

"That's what he called her?" asked Cameron, laughing.

"That was it. You ought to try it sometime and see what she says." Improvisational melodrama was Geoffrey's specialty.

"Right. Well, I think that's it for the storm. I suppose we should go down and let the cat out of the box," said Cameron.

"Good idea. If we're both standing there, he can't zip out of the box and escape."

Geoffrey opened the wooden door carefully, motioning for Cameron to be ready. Nothing happened. After a few seconds of silence, Geoffrey leaned down and peered into the box. "Kitty? Kitty? Oh my God!"

"What's the matter with him?"

"Nothing. He's happy as a clam at high tide. Oh my God. I'm doomed. I knew I shouldn't have quoted *Macbeth* this afternoon."

Cameron opened the door again and looked. There was Cluny in his tartan ribbon, surrounded by feathers, chewing contentedly on a sinewy bone.

"What is it?" whispered Geoffrey.

"Oh, fowls, absolutely," Cameron informed him. "See this bone here? There's been more than one of them, too. I'd say he's eaten them all."

Geoffrey put his hand to his brow. *"All? What, all my pretty chickens and their dam at one fell swoop?"*

"There you go again," said Cameron, recognizing the quote.

"The herding ducks! These things were going to be used in the sheepdog trials tomorrow. Elizabeth will kill me. How many were there?"

Cameron pulled on Cluny's lead, drawing the reluctant bobcat out of the box in a cloud of feathers. After a brief examination, he turned to Geoffrey: "Five, I think. All white—domestic ducks."

"Good," muttered Geoffrey. "Those shouldn't be too hard to find."

"Find?"

"Come on. I've got the car keys. But you have to promise not to tell anyone about this—especially not my cousin!"

Cameron trailed off after Geoffrey, the bobcat at his heels, wondering if duck-rustling was a hanging offense in the States these days. Coming to America seemed to be much akin to falling down a rabbit hole. . . .

"I think it's stopped raining," said Elizabeth. She was sitting on a campstool in the doorway of Marge Hutcheson's tent, with a mug of tea balanced in her lap.

"Finish your tea," said Marge. "Somerled doesn't need all that much practice." The border collie pricked up his ears at the sound of his name, and then stretched back out on the floor of the tent. His mistress—a hardy, gray-haired woman in tweeds and jodhpurs—rumpled his fur affectionately, "Nosy brute!"

"I expect I'm a nosy brute, too," said Elizabeth shyly. "But I was really shocked to hear about—you know—Dr. Hutcheson."

Marge grunted. "Poor Walter. Sometimes a dog will chase a truck just to prove he can keep up with it. I don't suppose they ever give any thought to what will happen if they catch it."

"What's she like? I guess I could find out for myself, since I was invited to their party tonight. But that was because of Cameron."

"Who's Cameron?"

Elizabeth sighed. "He's from Scotland."

"Not a very high recommendation with me nowadays," said Marge dryly.

"Oh, dear, I forgot. So is *she*. Dr. Hutcheson was bragging about her being the niece of the Duke of something . . . Rothesay?"

"The Earl of Rothes, I expect," said Marge. "He's the chief of Clan Leslie. Used to be in publishing."

"Umm . . . I thought he said Duke, but he may have got it wrong. He wasn't as up on those things as you are."

"No, Walter is a bit of a liability in everything except medicine. Still, this is the first I've heard of it, so he's sure to know more than I."

"Did you know her?"

Marge smiled. "We weren't best friends, dear. Somebody or other brought her to the country club once, and she managed to get Walter to give her golf lessons. I'm sure she plays much better than he does. Anyway, the first I heard of it was a few months later, when Walter decided that we weren't the same people we used to be and that he wanted to *find himself*." She shrugged. "We had Sanderson draw up the property settlement, and the divorce went through. I didn't even go to court for the occasion."

"That's terrible!" cried Elizabeth. "After all these years."

"I expect it's worse for Walter," said Marge complacently. "Imagine living with somebody who thinks of John Lennon as Julian Lennon's *dad*. Of course, Walter married her trying to feel young again, but I doubt if he's succeeding at it."

"Yes, but how do you feel?"

"I get by. I guess I feel most of the time as though someone has rearranged the furniture: you know, everything's familiar, but not quite right somehow. But I have the farm and the dogs, and I stay busy." She grinned. "I suppose you thought I ought to be after her with a pistol?"

Elizabeth blushed. "I didn't think I ought to go to the party. Because of you."

"Nonsense! And miss a chance to snoop? By all means go. You won't hurt my feelings a bit."

"Well . . . maybe Cameron will enjoy meeting another Scot."

"Perhaps. How long has he been here?"

Elizabeth burst out laughing. "All day!" she managed to say.

"Oh, right. Well, I doubt if he's quite that desperate for the company of his fellow countrymen, then. But by all means, go to the party. I take it you'd like an excuse to spend some more time with this young man?" Elizabeth nodded shyly. "Well, out with it! What's he like?"

"Very proper. And very witty in a deadpan sort of way. . . . Did I mention that he has a Ph.D. in marine biology? And he speaks BBC British with trilled *r*'s."

"Edinburgh," grunted Marge. "What is it, Somerled? Are you tired of being inside? Well, come on, then. I'll give you a walk. And as for you, young miss, you should go back to your cabin and get out of that stifling kilt getup. You'll feel much better in summer clothes."

"But I'm Maid of the Cat," Elizabeth protested.

Marge Hutcheson shrugged. "Please yourself. But if your Scottish fellow is anything like the Brits I know, he has a sense of smell like a blind bloodhound."

"I'm on my way!" cried Elizabeth, lunging for the door.

Walter Hutcheson, his ducal package still under his arm, was making the rounds of clan tents, making sure that he had invited all the chiefs to the party. Marge had always taken care of the inviting before, but Heather hardly knew anyone, so he couldn't expect her to do it. He hoped she would remember the ice this time. Heather was still learning the art of entertaining. Marge had made it seem so easy that he'd never given it much thought.

He wondered for the tenth time if he should have invited Marge: one heard so much these days about "civilized" divorces, but he would have been embarrassed as hell to have her present. Not that Marge would make a scene. Nothing ever seemed to upset her. But he kept imagining his former wife watching him and Heather at the party and being—in her quiet, well-bred way—quite amused. The thought of appearing ridiculous to someone as sensible as Marge troubled him when he allowed himself to consider it—which was not often, and never for long.

He banished the scene from his mind just as he came face-to-face with the one clan chief he had not intended to invite: Colin Campbell. Dr. Hutcheson's antipathy toward Colin lay not in the traditional MacDonald-Campbell feuds, but in the much more personal area of hospital politics, in which Dr. Campbell, by any other name, would still have been a pain in the ass. Since the games were a social event, Dr. Hutcheson tried to pass off their meeting with a cordial nod, but it was part of Colin Campbell's lack of charm that he never separated business from pleasure.

"So it's you, is it?" he growled, squinting at Walter. "What's this rubbish I hear about a personnel board?"

"Colin, there have been some complaints about you. Personally, I mean, not medically."

"Personally is nobody's business."

"Well, Colin, you know . . . You just put people's backs up. Like when you asked the young lady on 3B to get you some coffee and a doughnut."

"She's complaining about that?"

"She's a neurosurgeon."

"Well, she ought to see about her own nerves if she's as touchy as that. I don't see that it's worth calling a meeting over."

"No. Parkes said he waited until the complaint folder on you was too full to stay closed, and then he decided to convene. This one was just the final straw."

Dr. Campbell's eyes narrowed. "I suppose you volunteered to head this kangaroo court?"

"Somebody had to do it."

"Somebody's going to regret it, too," said Colin Campbell, his voice rising. "You know that lake property you've invested in? I'll bet you don't know who your fellow owners are."

"Nonsense, Colin. The university owns a good bit of the land." Walter Hutcheson sounded a bit shaken. His investments hadn't been going so well since Marge had turned it all over to him. She used to be phenomenally lucky.

"Don't forget that I'm a trustee, Walter. If we declare that lake a wildlife preserve, your little condo scheme is going straight down the tubes. And since my interest in marine biology is well known, no one's going to be too surprised when I suggest it."

"Colin, I doubt that a trustee—Anyway, you're talking about a lot of money here. A childish reaction, really. We both know that there's not a thing they can do to you, not even if they have a dozen meetings!"

"Childish am I? And I suppose you're the one who's going to send me to the principal's office? Well, I hope you get your money's worth."

Dr. Hutcheson didn't realize that he was shouting. "If you ruin this lake project for me, I'll see you in hell, *doctor!*"

A woman in a Logan tartan shied and hurried away. Honestly, she thought, the real ones are as bad as on *General Hospital.*

Colin Campbell ambled along the row of clan tents humming contentedly to himself. Quite a lot of the Campbells were inclined to forget the age-old feuds between the clans and to behave like everybody else at these festivals, but Colin believed in keeping the traditions alive. It relieved the monotony of life, for one thing. Colin didn't like people, as a rule, which might seem strange for a physician, but actually the two were not incompatible. Colin Campbell rarely thought of his patients as people: they were anatomical projects. He worked on them as a jackleg mechanic might tinker with cars, and he didn't trouble himself over whether he liked them individually. There were exceptions, of course. Colin Campbell liked *some* people very well indeed, but they were merely the exceptions proving the rule. Having been thoroughly objectionable to everyone all afternoon, thus upholding the Campbell reputation, Colin was treating himself to a visit with one of his few friends.

He found her in the practice meadow walking her border collie.

"Always dogs!" he chided her. "Don't you ever associate with people?"

"I'm fond of beasts!" Marge Hutcheson called back. "And you qualify. Want to walk with us?"

"I might as well. I've just had a run-in with that husband of yours, and I need to work off steam."

Marge raised her eyebrows. "I assume you mean Walter."

"I said your husband, didn't I?" He flushed. "Oh, sorry. I forgot that he's been even more of a damned fool than usual. Anyway, the bit of fluff is such a nonentity that I keep forgetting she exists."

Marge smiled. "Colin, you old liar! I'll bet you haven't even met her."

"Well, who says I have to? When a man of Walter's age makes a fool of himself over a skinny teenager—"

"Oh, Colin, stop blustering. I'll bet you've been at it all day."

"Pretty well." He grinned.

"Get anyone's goat?"

"Fair to middling. That Maid of the Cat accused me of

being in drag."

"Served you right, you old bully! I'll bet you liked her for it, too."

"No respect for her elders," he grunted.

"That's my friend Elizabeth MacPherson, so you leave her alone. And what have you been after Walter about? Not his marital status, surely."

"No. He's trying to convene some lynch mob against me at the hospital, so I threatened to hit him where it hurts: in the pocketbook!"

"You're going to sue him?"

"Nah! Then the lawyers get all the fun. I'm going to see that he loses a bundle on that lakefront property he bought. Get it zoned against condos."

"Colin, you really are incorrigible." Marge shook her head. "How is Walter doing in his investments, anyway?"

"How do you think? You were the only one with a grain of sense about it. Clever of you to hand them over to him. I doubt if he'll be able to afford his childbride at the rate he's going."

"Well, I expect she has money of her own, if it isn't tied up in Scotland."

"Scotland?"

"See!" cried Marge triumphantly. "I knew you hadn't met her! Colin, you really should behave so that people would invite you places. You'd learn so much more that way."

"Scotland, eh? What's he done, found Flora Mac-Donald?"

"Better than that, from what I hear. Walter says she's the niece of a Scottish nobleman."

Colin Campbell grunted. "Some of those lords are poorer

than schoolteachers."

"That's what I said." Marge nodded. "But Elizabeth is sure Walter said he was a duke."

Colin Campbell snorted. "The only duke Walter knows is the university in Durham. Lousy basketball team!"

"Oh, leave poor Walter alone." Marge sighed. "What's done is done. Why don't you tell me what you've been up to? You still have that ugly brute of a bulldog?"

They walked off together down one of the Glencoe Mountain nature trails, too far from the festival grounds for the participants to be startled by the sound of Colin Campbell—laughing.

CHAPTER SIX

"A Doctorate in biology is not required to keep ducks in a cardboard box," said Cameron between clenched teeth.

"No, but in order to drive a car, one must remember which side of the road to drive on," said Geoffrey sweetly. "How are the ducks?"

"They're huddled in the box, saying cheep, cheep, cheep."

"They're lying, then. They cost me six bucks apiece. The problem is, how are we going to smuggle them into the herding box?"

Cameron raised his eyebrows. "We? I'm supposed to meet Elizabeth soon."

"That's true. I do want to make sure she's distracted. You can take her the cat, too."

"How do I explain that?"

"Tell her the truth. Tell her you're giving me advice

about *Brigadoon.* Just don't mention ducks. Is this our turnoff—at the church?"

"Yes!" called Cameron. "First Assembly of God." He laughed. "I suppose they put the chrome and wheels on elsewhere."

Geoffrey nodded approvingly. "Elizabeth's taste in men is improving."

Cameron, who had heard his share of Southern feud stories and been warned about America's tendency toward firearms, said uneasily, "Of course, my . . . um . . . intentions toward her are strictly honorable."

Geoffrey hooted. "You're on your own, then. I'm not vouching for Elizabeth."

Lachlan Forsyth was straightening his rack of books on Scotland. No one ever put things back where they found them; but then the stall was so crowded, maybe they couldn't reach the same spot twice. Jimmy's parents had come and collected him for a dinner break, with wistful references to another party they'd been asked to, so Lachlan had offered to have the boy back through the Hill-Sing. He was a bright enough lad, and more help than trouble. Lachlan was that glad of the company, he might knock a bit off the hundred-per-cent profit he'd be making on the *skian dubh.*

A beefy man in an old-style wrap kilt rested his leather shield on the scarf display. Lachlan, thinking he looked familiar, edged closer.

"Stands Scotland where it did?" whispered the man.

"Alas, poor country!" said Lachlan solemnly. *"Almost afraid to know itself!"*

70

"Right," said the bearded man with a sigh of relief. "I'm a Wylie of Clan Gunn. Are we having a meeting here at the games?"

"We'll risk it, laddie. And there'll be a sign."

"Good. Listen, how's it going? I keep scanning *Newsweek* for car-bombings in Edinburgh, but so far nothing's happening."

"Which is as it should be," Lachlan assured him. "Do you want a lot of commotion in the country like they have in Ireland, tipping the world off to what we're planning? There's nae strategy in that, is there? We're stockpiling our weapons and waiting to do it all in one fell swoop."

Wylie frowned. "How do you know the ordinary people will go along with it?"

"Ah, do you remember a few years ago when the Stone of Scone was stolen from Westminster Abbey?"

"Scone . . . That's the thing you need at the coronation in order to be King of Scotland." Lachlan nodded. "But they got it back."

"Laddie, they *think* they got it back."

Wylie of Gunn gasped. "So the Cause has the means to crown a Scottish king. Where is it? The Stone, I mean."

Lachlan Forsyth hesitated. "At Tarbert," he whispered. He was always afraid that sooner or later someone would point out that there were four places on the map of Scotland labeled Tarbert, but so far no one had caught on.

Wylie frowned. "I've been thinking about this earldom business, Mr. Forsyth. You know—getting a castle and all for helping to sponsor the revolution. And it seems to me that it would cost a pretty fair bit of money to keep up one of them things, wouldn't it?"

Lachlan played his trump card. "Why, laddie, when we pull out of Great Britain and set up the republic—who do you think will get the North Sea oil rights?"

His co-conspirator grinned. "Outstanding! One last thing, though. You're not letting any of these Campbells into this, are you?"

"What do you think?" said Lachlan slyly.

"Good. I reckon when we take over, we can pay them back for the Glencoe Massacre, and Culloden, and all the rest of it."

"Spot on!" murmured Lachlan. God, these Americans are a bloodthirsty lot, he thought as the man sauntered away. One of them had even offered him some back issues of *Mercenary Times* so that he could order grenade launchers. At moments like these, Lachlan found it easy to convince himself that he was a hero for taking people's money. At least he saw that they did nae harm with it. "Wise men buy and sell, and fools are bought and sold," he said aloud. It was his favorite line from Walter Scott.

Elizabeth, wearing a white sundress and sandals, looked considerably cooler and more self-possessed than she had before, but Cameron was too tired to care. He handed over Cluny's leash, saying that he had run into Geoffrey and volunteered to take Cluny off his hands.

"Where is Geoffrey?" asked Elizabeth, looking around.

"Oh . . . he went off with some friends," said Cameron vaguely. "He'll catch up with us later, I expect."

Elizabeth frowned. "Okay. Well, would you like to go to the Hutchesons' party? His new wife is Scottish, so I thought you might like to meet her."

"That might prove interesting," said Cameron politely. And if she's normal, he thought, then I can rule out the water-supply theory and assume that American insanity is genetic.

"Do you know that man over there?" asked Elizabeth. "The one in the red kilt with the leather shield. He seems to be staring at you."

"I can't think why," murmured Cameron. "There are certainly enough oddities in this place without him—"

"Shhh! Here he comes!"

The husky warrior nodded to Elizabeth and, drawing close to Cameron, he hissed, "Couldn't help noticing your accent as I went by, friend."

Cameron winced. The man had a voice like an untuned banjo. "Oh, yes?" he murmured, edging away.

The stranger fixed him with a piercing stare. "Tell me," he said hoarsely. *"Stands Scotland where it did?"*

Another loony. And this one was wearing a sword the size of a horse's leg. Cameron giggled nervously.

"Stands Scotland where it did!" the man repeated in menacing tones.

"Ye-ees," stammered Cameron. "Fifty-eight degrees north latitude, more or less. Go to Newcastle and turn left—"

"You'd better learn the right answer, buddy," the stranger drawled. "It could save your life someday."

Elizabeth watched him stalk off, the claymore swinging at his side. "What was that all about?" she whispered.

"I think it was a geography quiz," said Cameron wonderingly.

Geoffrey took a roundabout way to the herding-practice

73

meadow, reasoning that a quacking cardboard box might be hard to explain to the festival folks. There was no one in sight. With a last furtive glance toward the field path, Geoffrey scurried down the hill and set his container next to the wooden herding box.

"Fair is foul, and foul is fair," he muttered, scooping out bones and feathers. After a quick wipe with his only cotton handkerchief, he shoved the replacement ducks into their new quarters and scooped the evidence of their predecessors into his cardboard box.

Voices—from the woodland nature trail. Geoffrey froze.

They would be rounding the bend at any moment. Too late to run. Geoffrey stashed the cardboard box behind the stack of boards and stood up.

"It still doesn't sound quite right," Colin Campbell was saying. "I think I'll check on it."

"Please yourself. I—here!" Marge thundered. "What are you doing by the herding props?"

"I thought I heard a noise," said Geoffrey, brushing dried grass from his pants leg. "A rat after the duck food, perhaps."

"Nonsense," snapped Marge. "Aren't any rats out here. Now run along."

Geoffrey strolled away in the direction of the festival. He hoped that she wouldn't be around when someone finally opened the cardboard box.

Elizabeth stole a glance at Cameron. So much for the myth that Scots were short and stocky. *I could have worn my heels,* she thought wistfully.

"So many tartans!" Cameron was saying. "Wars must

have been confusing in the old days. Can you see a guy charging at someone on the battlefield, and he's thumbing through a wee book, saying, 'Blue plaid, one vertical white stripe and two green ones. Ah . . . here it is. He's an enemy. Aiiii!' "

Elizabeth laughed. "Silly! How did they really do it?"

"Haven't the foggiest. Never did much history. But if you want to know anything at all about seals—"

"No thanks. Not even to hear you trill your *r*'s. Anyway, we're here. There's the MacDonald banner."

"Ummm. Must be half the bloody clan on the lawn, too. Now, who are these people again?"

"The Hutchesons. My friend Marge is our host's ex-wife. And he wants you to meet his present wife, who's from Scotland. Does that make sense?"

Cameron sighed. "It does today."

They threaded their way through the crowd to a redwood picnic table laden with bottles and plastic cups. Behind it Walter Hutcheson was acting as impromptu bartender. He was still wearing his kilt, belted half plaid, and wool Prince Charlie coatee. The MacDonald clan badge on his Balmoral flashed in the lamplight. He eyed Cameron's less formal attire with a superior smile, and Cameron grinned back.

"Hello, Elizabeth," he said pleasantly. "You're old enough to drink, aren't you? . . . And you must be our visiting Scot. What can I get for you?"

"Straight Scotch—no ice," said Cameron.

The camper door opened, and a tiny blonde appeared, carrying a stack of napkins. She was easily the most elegant person there, in a long dress of white silk offset by a diamond pendant. "I might as well be wearing a feed sack," thought Elizabeth. The new wife looked very aristocratic indeed.

"Heather, dear, I've found you another Scot!" said Walter, helping her down. "Now don't you bother with her title, young man. You're in a democratic country now. My wife, Heather Hutcheson, this is . . ." Dr. Hutcheson's voice trailed away. He was staring beyond them into the crowd. "Well . . . good land. What's he doing here? Excuse me."

He edged through the throng and disappeared. After a few moments of awkward silence, Cameron introduced himself and Elizabeth.

"Batair didn't tell me there was another Scot about," said Heather, frowning. "Where's your home?"

"Edinburgh."

She smiled. "Aren't Americans funny? They think just because we come from the same effing country, it ought to be straight in, cup o'tea, feet under the table—Ke-rist, what's that?"

"He's the Chattan mascot," said Cameron, pointing to Cluny just as the bobcat rubbed his back against Heather's legs.

"Eeee!" she cried. "What did you want to bring a sodding *animal* for? This party is dead posh! . . . Ooo, what a ming! Is it the cat or your bird there?"

Cameron's jaw tightened. Elizabeth looked around for the bird. "So you have a title," he said smoothly. "You know, I'll bet you come from a dear green place in the west."

Heather smiled. "And you're Clan Sloane, of course."

"Did you two go to school together?" asked Elizabeth, to

whom the conversation made very little sense.

"I went to Fettes," said Cameron. "How about you?"

"Park."

"Oh. Bellahouston?"

Elizabeth, who was still lost, smiled and tried to look intelligent, despite no one's paying her any mind. "Is Bella-what's-it a college?"

"Been here long?" asked Heather, ignoring her.

"No. Just arrived."

"Fast work. Shagged the scrubber yet, Jimmy?"

Elizabeth seized on a familiar word. "Jimmy? Is that your nickname, Cameron?"

"Sometimes," said Cameron softly. "And her ladyship's nickname is Senga."

"She sounds much more Scottish than you do," Elizabeth remarked. "Such a wonderful accent."

"Oh, toffee-noses talk like the Beeb," said Heather.

Cameron sighed. "Look: if there are no further strikes on Morningside, the Gorbals will be safe as well. Got it, Senga?"

Heather shrugged. "Fair enough, Jimmy."

"Right. We'll be off, then, your ladyship." Cameron turned to Elizabeth. "Come on, hen."

When they were out of earshot, Elizabeth said, "At first I thought she was mad at you because you didn't treat her like one of the nobility. Then I got really confused. I guess you got along okay, though." She sniffed. "After all, you called *her* your ladyship, and *me,* hen."

Cameron smiled. "You got the best of it, lassie."

Walter Hutcheson tried not to look worried as he maneuvered his way toward the uninvited guest. He hoped that Colin hadn't come to continue their argument about the lake property.

"Evening, Colin," he said cautiously. "Can I get you a drink?"

Colin Campbell scowled at the party in general. "Oh, why not?" he grumbled. "As long as you don't go off playing the host. I need your attention for once."

"Is anything the matter?" asked Dr. Hutcheson in his professional voice. He couldn't think of a likelier candidate for a stroke.

Dr. Campbell followed his host back to the picnic table, trying to converse over recorded bagpipe music. "Now, you know we don't always get along, Walter," he said in an urgent undertone. "But the one thing we have no problem with is *fraud*. Remember that resident at the hospital who turned out to have a medical degree from a matchbook? You were on my side about that fast enough."

"Well, of course, Colin," said Dr. Hutcheson mildly. "It was a matter of ethics, for the good of the organization, and all that. Why?"

"Exactly. I came to tell you that we need to call a meeting of the festival committee first thing tomorrow. There's something extraordinary going on. I happened on to it by chance."

"Here you are, Batair," Heather pouted. "Why did you go off and leave me with that prat and his bird? And we're nearly out of ice, as well."

"Sorry, dear," he murmured. "I just need to have a word with Dr. Campbell. Colin, may I present my wife, Heather."

"How do you do?" said Colin stiffly. "I've heard of you."

Heather turned on her new husband. "Oh, Batair! Have you been telling folk about my family connections again? You promised you wouldn't! I don't want to be treated any different."

"Heather, I didn't—"

"That sort of secret doesn't keep," said Colin with a sour smile. "I found it very interesting. I believe you're to be congratulated on a new cousin."

"What?"

"Your uncle, the Duke. Once again a proud father, I believe."

Heather frowned. "You know him?"

Dr. Campbell remained noncommittal. "I mustn't take up the hostess's time with family chitchat. You'll have to see to your guests. But sometime we might talk about it."

"Colin is quite a hobbyist in genealogy," Dr. Hutcheson remarked. "Now, what was it you wanted to see me about?"

"Oh, the fraud business? Perhaps we ought to wait until the committee assembles in the morning. I'll have the materials with me then. It'll save time."

"Look," said Heather, "do you want a drink?"

"What are you having?" asked Colin Campbell. "Babycham?"

He was still laughing as he walked away.

CHAPTER SEVEN

Glencoe Mountain loomed dark against the sky. In the light of a quarter-moon, the stalls and clan tents stood as empty as a stage set of *Brigadoon*; but farther along the field path, in the herding meadow, the festival folk were preparing for the Hill-Sing. An hour after sunset, members of the clans began to line up for the ceremony, while the spectators spread their tartan blankets down on the meadow and hillside in preparation for the evening's festivities.

"This is a lovely ceremony," Elizabeth whispered to Cameron. "Watch."

One by one, a kilted representative from each clan ran across the field, holding aloft a burning torch. When all of the clansmen stood on the field, the torches formed a Cross of St. Andrew that they held in flickering silence for a few moments, followed by wild cheering from the spectators in the darkness.

"Yes, that was quite nice," said Cameron. "What happens next?"

Elizabeth pointed to a dark shape in the center of the field. As the cheering died away, each torchbearer laid his firebrand on the stack of logs, igniting it into a roaring blaze. From the shadows a tenor voice sang the first line of "Annie Laurie," and one by one other voices joined in from all sections of the field.

"Do you know this one?" whispered Elizabeth.

"What do you mean do I know this one?" Cameron hissed back. "It's a Scottish song! We bloody wrote it! Of course I—Well, I'm a bit hazy on the verses, though."

Elizabeth joined in for the chorus. By the time they had sung it twice, she had noticed that "Cameron Dawson" had almost the same number of syllables as "Annie Laurie"; and while she was careful to sing the words correctly, there was unusual fervor in her rendering of "lay me doon and dee."

Cameron began to feel relaxed for the first time all day. The soothing sounds of a familiar song, mingled with the darkness and the beauty of the mountain setting, made him feel that the trip hadn't been such a waste after all. He smiled at Elizabeth, and reached down to pet the sleeping bobcat. Somehow it was all beginning to make sense.

Jimmy McGowan stared into the flames of the bonfire, thankful that his parents were not around to foist marshmallows off on him. Beside him, Lachlan Forsyth was leaning forward and swinging on his cane in time to the music.

"That's the only good song they'll sing tonight, lad," he roared as the crowd struggled with the high note with varying degrees of success. "From here on out, they won't half come out with some rubbish."

A voice across the meadow began to bellow: *"You take the high road, and I'll take the low road!"*

"I've heard this one," said Jimmy.

"Sung just like that, I'll wager," growled Lachlan. "Folk should nae sing a tune if they haven't any idea what it means. Listen to them belting it out like they were singing about a bloody hiking competition!"

"And I'll be in Scotland before ya!" roared the crowd.

"But me and my true love will never meet again . . ."

"What does it mean?" asked Jimmy.

"It's a Jacobite song from the '45," Lachlan said. "When Charles Edward Stuart—"

Jimmy recognized the name. "Bonnie Prince Charlie?"

The old man grunted. "He was nae bonny, and nae much of a prince, but he was a right bloody Charlie. Anyway, he and his Highland army invaded England, and this song is about a Scottish soldier dying. He says for his mates to take the high road—the highway—back to Scotland, and he'll take the low road, which is the way the fairy folk travel— in a twinkling of an eye."

Jimmy nodded. "So he'll be in Scotland before them because he's using magic."

"Aye, but it won't profit him any to get there, because he'll not be meeting his sweetheart again, being dead like he is."

"On the bonny, bonny banks of Loch Lomond . . ."

Jimmy was still thinking about the prince. His parents were always bragging about a McGowan ancestor who'd fought with him, and how Jimmy ought to be proud to wear a kilt in his honor. "My parents want me to get a kilt," he told Lachlan. He explained about his Jacobite ancestor, and the old man listened, shaking his head. "Do you think I ought to let them buy me one?"

The voices on the hill had begun to croon "The Bluebells of Scotland."

"Ah, your braw McGowan ancestor," sighed Lachlan. "Let me tell you how it was, laddie, as if you was him."

James Stuart McGowan pictured himself astride a white horse, wearing the red and black Gow tartan, sword at his

82

side. Too cool, he thought.

"April 16, 1746 . . . and the Highland army under his right bloody Charlie is waiting to meet the English at Culloden Field. McGowan. He wasn't a clan chief. Nobody very important. Say he was a subtenant. So part of the rent for his little piece of land was that he had to go and fight when he was told to, or else have his house burned over his head and his one cow killed. He might have been quite young—say fourteen."

"Did he have a horse?" asked Jimmy.

Lachlan laughed. "He did not. And nae food, either. They left the food back in Inverness by mistake. And brought the wrong size ammunition for the cannon, as well."

"What about a sword?"

"Oh, aye, a bloody great claymore ye canna lift. And waiting for you across the field is a well-fed English army led by the Duke of Cumberland—Stinking Billy, he was—and they've got loaded muskets, bayonets, and cannons with grapeshot."

Jimmy shivered. "*Swords* against muskets and bayonets?"

"Aye. So there you are, McGowan of the prince's army. You're cold and ragged; you have nae eaten for three days n'er slept for twa, and you did nae want to come and fight in the first place, but the laird said you had to. And you're holding a sword ye canna lift while looking down the barrel of a bloody musket, or at an army of grinning faces who'll bayonet you on the field if you don't die during the battle. Aye. Sounds a treat, doesn't it, Jimmy? And McGowan of Clan Gow is thinking tae himself. 'If I can stay alive long enough to get off this sodding field, I'll get me out of Scotland and ship out to whatever godforsaken colony will have me, and please God that I never see that stinking tartan of my landlord's ever again.'"

"What a stupid war," grumbled Jimmy.

"Well, don't go blaming McGowan for it. Sometimes I think of the likes of him, though, in some celestial distillery looking down on his descendants parading around in that great bloody tartan that got him killed, and I think how fash't he'd be with you."

"Then why do people make such a big deal out of it?" asked Jimmy.

"Because people like to think that glory and honor existed in the world somewhere, sometime, and that it has aught to do with them." He sighed. "I don't suppose they do any harm, though."

Jimmy didn't answer. He was listening to the wail of a bagpipe somewhere in the distance, and trying to imagine how it would feel to walk into the crossfire of an army.

"I always cry at this one," said Elizabeth, dabbing her eyes. "'The Bluebells of Scotland.' When they say, 'O where and o where is your Highland laddie gone?' I always think he must have been killed in the war."

"War?"

"Oh, yes. In Charlie's year, when the Highland clans fought the English. For Bonnie Prince Charlie."

"Is he popular over here? I saw Princess Diana in a parade once."

"You *don't* mean you've never heard of Charles Edward Stuart?" said Elizabeth menacingly.

"Oh, him. Of course I have. I think I had to do a report

on him once."

"Isn't it sad that the Rising failed?" sighed Elizabeth. "If only they hadn't had such bad luck—"

"Yes, but then we'd be out of the United Kingdom," said Cameron reasonably. "And that would simply kill the economy. It would set us back forty years industrially."

Elizabeth shook her head. She couldn't see what economics could have to do with such a just and noble cause as the Stuarts' right to the throne. Men had such odd ways of looking at things. But, she thought, snuggling closer to Cameron, it didn't seem worth fighting about this late in the day.

As a student of theatre, Geoffrey thought that the Hill-Sing had the most dramatic potential of anything that had happened thus far. He wondered if he could incorporate something similar into the second act of *Brigadoon*. He was just trying to decide what kind of lighting it would take to get the shadows right, when a single voice began a new song.

"Flower of Scotland, when will we see your like again . . ."

Geoffrey noticed that several people about the field were struggling to their feet and standing at attention. Must be another of their rituals, he thought. Might as well go along with it. Geoffrey stood respectfully, straining to catch the words. Something about "proud Edward's army." History, he supposed.

By the time the singers had reached the last verse, most of the people at the Hill-Sing were standing, out of some obscure instinct to follow the leader.

"Those days are passed now, And in the past they must remain . . ."

"They're dead right about that," muttered Lachlan Forsyth in another part of the field.

Near the bonfire, Jerry Buchanan wiped a tear from under his glasses and sang on lustily. So many people standing—the Cause was growing.

The last notes of the Corries' song were still hanging in the air when a stocky man in a kilt eased in beside Geoffrey and said in a solemn undertone: *"Stands Scotland where it did?"*

Hello! thought Geoffrey. Another theatre person. Act four, scene three. In his best Shakespearean tones, Geoffrey rounded on the man and proclaimed: *"Alas, poor country! Almost afraid to know itself! It cannot be called our mother but our grave . . ."* Then, dropping his pose, he said cheerfully, "There! We've quoted from the Scottish tragedy and we're both damned. Quick— turn round three times and swear!"

The man shook his head. "You must outrank me, friend," he drawled. "I just know the ordinary password. Anyhow, I'd like to invite you to a little get-together some of us are having."

"A party?" asked Geoffrey hopefully.

"Yep. You don't even have to bring your own bottle, seeing as how you're one of the big-shots. Follow me, sir."

The mention of bottles combined with Geoffrey's natural curiosity to make him follow the man without further discussion. This is interesting, he thought. He managed to resist the temptation to say, *"Lay on, Macduff."*

His new acquaintance led him to a large motor home in

the camping area. Inside, half a dozen men in different plaids were seated at a plastic table examining a map of Scotland.

"The boss will be here soon," said a man in a green kilt and a cowboy hat. "He had a kid with him, and he's waiting for the parents to come back."

"I found another one of the higher-ups," said the stocky man, pointing to Geoffrey. "He's an American, too. Don't it beat all? I ran across a real Scotsman at the clan tents today, and he didn't know jackshit about any of this."

"No, you mustn't mention this to him," said Geoffrey quickly. "He's MI5—British secret service." He was most gratified by his audience's startled gasps. This is like improvisational drama, Geoffrey thought cheerfully. I wonder what I'll say next.

"Should we get him out of the way?" asked one of the men in carefully neutral tones.

Whoops—dangerous ad-libbing, thought Geoffrey. I don't want to get Cameron mugged by this bunch of . . . whatever they are. "Absolutely not," he said solemnly. "That would attract too much attention. It's best to ignore him. Do you suppose I could have a drink?"

"Well . . . we usually wait for the boss, but seeing as how you're obviously somebody important . . ." He indicated Geoffrey's Royal Stewart necktie.

One of the men got out plastic cups and a bottle of Drambuie, while another set a small bowl of water in the center of the table. When the cups had been filled, the men held them above the water bowl. A little nervously, Geoffrey followed suit.

"To the king over the water!" they intoned.

Geoffrey, who had spent the last few moments contemplating his necktie and reading the back of the Drambuie bottle, had begun to make sense of things. Charles Stuart again, he thought, noting that the Bonnie Prince was credited with the original recipe of the liqueur. A man of many talents, Geoffrey decided: bootlegger, female impersonator—it seemed churlish to quibble about his generalship. Besides, he had been dead for nearly two centuries; but not, apparently, resting in peace. Surely these clowns couldn't be contemplating the overthrow of the British government.

"And success to the Scottish Republican Army!" cried the man in the cowboy hat.

Or could they?

Lachlan Forsyth appeared in the doorway, his genial smile fading a bit when he noticed Geoffrey among the kilted conspirators. "Evening, lads," he said softly.

"Hello," said Geoffrey quickly. "I think you've done a splendid job with the recruits here."

Lachlan looked at him speculatively. "Oh, aye?"

"Even so, I haven't disclosed any of the military strategy. I feel that the fewer people who know, the better, don't you?"

Lachlan nodded. "Perhaps we might have a wee talk later," he murmured, easing into a chair.

"Oh, absolutely. How about a drink? A little Scotch, perhaps?" Geoffrey was particularly good at parties.

The Hill-Sing bonfire had burned low, and many of the festival participants had picked up their blankets and straggled off toward the campgrounds. Elizabeth, who did not want the evening to end, was giving her best imitation of someone who was still awake.

She sighed. "I love Scottish folk music."

Since the last song had been "Home on the Range," Cameron was at a loss for a reply. "It's after midnight," he said softly. "Do you think your cousin will be worried about you?"

Elizabeth took a deep breath. "No," she said. "But having them drag the river for my body would be his idea of a joke. Perhaps we'd better get back."

"The stars are very nice up here," Cameron remarked as they walked along the trail. "You can see a lot more of them here than you can in Edinburgh."

Elizabeth stifled a yawn. "I'd rather see them in Edinburgh."

"Just don't expect it to be anything like this," Cameron warned her. "Over there, if you see someone walking down Princes Street in a full kilt, it's bound to be an American."

"So, what is a Scot?" mused Elizabeth sleepily. "Someone with a pedigree back to the Duke of Somebody or someone who knows all the dances and songs and customs? Or somebody like you, who doesn't know any of it, but who has a passport to prove he's Scottish?" She looked up at him for an answer and promptly tripped over a rock.

"I don't know," said Cameron, catching her. "But people who get philosophical at one in the morning while stumbling over rocks are always assumed to be Irish."

"Close enough," murmured Elizabeth, suiting her actions to the words; and Cameron had one brief flash of anxiety before he discovered that, despite their other cultural aberrations, Americans were perfectly sound in the matter of kissing.

89

Some time later, they reached the porch of Elizabeth's cabin; all was dark. "Good night," said Cameron, kissing the Maid of the Cat. "Thanks for a lovely evening."

Elizabeth smiled. "Be thankful I remembered where the rock was."

"I'll see you tomorrow," laughed Cameron as he started down the steps. "I'd better—good God!"

"What's wrong, Cameron?"

"I haven't seen the Carsons since four o'clock. I have no idea where I'm going."

Elizabeth took a deep breath. "You can stay here," she said in a small voice.

Cameron hesitated. "Well, I suppose I could, if you wouldn't mind. Is there a couch or something?" he asked, following her in.

Quite amazingly dim, thought Elizabeth. I wonder, do unicorns follow him at a respectful distance?

Cameron flipped on the light. "No couch. Ah, is that Geoffrey's room? Perhaps he wouldn't mind?" Before Elizabeth could phrase her opinion that Cameron would be safer with her, he had tried the bedroom door and found it locked. "Should we try to wake him?"

Elizabeth picked up an empty Drambuie bottle from under the chair. "Not a hope," she said cheerfully.

"Oh! Well, there's always the floor. Do you have an extra blanket?"

"I don't take up much room," said Elizabeth softly, pointing to the double bed.

Steady on, Cameron told himself. This country was getting more interesting by the minute. "Right," he said aloud. "Is that the bathroom? I'm going to take a shower.

Be right back."

"I think there are towels in there," Elizabeth said.

I'll probably be shaking too hard to need one, Cameron thought, closing the door behind him. Twenty minutes later he emerged from the bathroom wearing his khaki shorts (discretion being the better part of valor) to find the bedroom dark. The light from the bathroom illuminated the bed, though, so that he could see Elizabeth snuggled against her pillow, still dressed, sound asleep. On the other side of the bed sprawled Cluny the bobcat, watching Cameron with unblinking yellow eyes. Cameron didn't feel like making its day: he was too tired. He picked up the small tartan blanket they'd used at the Hill-Sing, flipped out the bathroom light, and curled up in the armchair beside the dresser. Considering how the day had gone, he didn't know why he'd expected anything else. Selkies, sea serpents, loonies asking where Scotland stood. This wasn't a country, it was a bloody roller-coaster.

From the darkness a drowsy voice said, "Are you going to stay in that damned chair all night?"

CHAPTER EIGHT

"O where and o where is your Highland laddie gone?"

Elizabeth opened her eyes. There it was again. "The Bluebells of Scotland" being sung by . . . Geoffrey? She squinted at the sunlight streaming through the window. Impossible. Geoffrey would never sing a Scottish folk song; tunes from *Threepenny Opera* were more his style. And where was Cameron? She looked around. Cluny was curled on a blanket in the armchair, still asleep; of

Cameron there was no sign.

"*. . . is your Highland laddie gone . . .*"

Elizabeth, now wide awake, finally got the message. Scrunching down under the covers, she called out, "Yes, Geoffrey! My Highland laddie is gone! You can come out now!"

A blue-robed form sped past and slammed the bathroom door. "And don't use all the hot water!" Elizabeth called after him.

Some time later, Elizabeth, in a strapless yellow sundress, was towel-drying her hair while Geoffrey made coffee in the electric percolator.

"How was your evening, cousin?" he asked pleasantly.

Elizabeth looked up suspiciously. "Why do you ask?"

"Just making conversation, dear. I am a notoriously sound sleeper, you know. Nothing disturbs me."

"Then what prompted you to ask if my Highland laddie were gone?" she demanded. "You were asleep when we got back."

"Call of nature about four A.M.," Geoffrey murmured. "Do you want any of this powdered stuff in your coffee?"

"Cameron forgot to find out where his hosts were staying," said Elizabeth, blushing.

"I wish I had the sort of mooncalf manner that could pull off a line like that," said Geoffrey wistfully. "People always seem to suspect me of ulterior motives, no matter how subtle I've been."

"And I know how you spent your evening," said Elizabeth, pointing to the empty bottle in the wastebasket. "Up to no good, as usual."

"On the contrary," Geoffrey retorted. "I was made the

Earl of Strathclyde last night."

As Walter Hutcheson turned the corner with sausage rolls and coffee balanced on a cardboard tray, he nearly collided with his wife. Heather was not looking particularly Scottish in her gold metallic Chinese sheath with the slit sides, but she thought that the sexiness of the outfit more than compensated; the stiletto heels gave her much-needed extra height and complemented her legs, as well. "Up early, aren't you?" she said.

"Thought I'd get us some breakfast. I was looking for Colin, too. He said something about wanting a committee meeting this morning."

Heather scowled. "What a tiresome old bampot he is. You're not going to go off all day, are you?"

"No. I just thought I might see him. Shall we go and sit down?"

Heather followed him to one of the picnic tables under the refreshment tent without noticeable enthusiasm. She made a face at the sausage rolls and reached for one of the coffees.

Walter glanced uneasily at his wife's diamond earrings and pendant, then returned his gaze to his own cup. Was it Scott Fitzgerald who said "The rich are different from you and me"? So was the aristocracy, he thought with a heavy heart. He imagined people taking Heather's costume at face value—and of course assuming that the diamonds were rhinestones, which they most certainly were not.

"That's not very . . . ethnic," he said gently.

Heather's eyes widened. "Not *ethnic?* Chinese is about as bloody ethnic as it comes."

"But, honey, you're not Chinese."

"Well, there's not many Scots about up here, is there? But you don't see it stopping them from wearing kilts."

"That reminds me. One of the folks running a souvenir booth is a Scotsman, and he'd like very much to meet you."

Heather frowned. "And why is that?"

"I believe I may have mentioned your family connections."

"Oh, Batair, sod off."

"He's a nice old fellow. White hair and a beard, bit red in the face. Has hypertension, I wouldn't doubt," he said, lapsing into his professional manner. "I bought that tartan scarf from him, and he was most helpful."

"I know who you mean. Perhaps I'll stop and have a natter with him later."

"That's my girl." Walter smiled. "Well, it's nearly time for the sheepdog events. I think I'll go over and take a look at them. Want to come?"

"I'll join you in a bit," said Heather. She had not forgotten that the principal exhibitor in the dog trials was Batair's former wife.

Lachlan Forsyth smiled at the blushing young lady in the yellow sundress. "Now what would you be wanting to know a thing like that for? 'I love you' in Gaelic, is it? Fancy!"

"Oh . . . I was just interested," murmured Elizabeth, turning a deeper shade of red. "Don't you know how to say it?"

"Oh, aye. But it'll no do you any good tae learn it."

Seeing her stricken look, he said gently, "I mean because of your young man, lassie. He's from Edinburgh. He doesna know Gaelic from oregano, and doesn't care to learn. If you really want to impress him, forget about that Celtic rubbish and learn to hold your fork in your left hand—so you don't have to switch the cutlery round when you're using the knife. Look out now, company's coming."

Elizabeth turned and saw Geoffrey and Cameron heading toward the stall. She wondered if she was still blushing.

"Ah," said Geoffrey. "I see you've met my friend, the Thane of Cawdor, Elizabeth. And look who I found. He was at the refreshment tent, trying to order a hot dog with lettuce and tomato. Said he wanted to try American food."

"Apparently I still need a guide," said Cameron to Elizabeth. "Are you still available?" Elizabeth nodded, with an expression best described as simpering.

"Run along now, children!" said Geoffrey briskly. "All this honey and pancake syrup is making Uncle Geoffie queasy."

"Let's go and see the sheepdog trials," murmured Elizabeth.

"What are they charged with?" asked Cameron.

"Dog trials! Perhaps I'd better go with you," said Geoffrey. "Got to run, Lachlan. Catch you later!"

"Don't be too sure of that, lad," muttered Lachlan when they were gone.

"Is everything okay?" asked James Stuart, at his elbow. "You been acting kind of funny today."

"Oh, fine, lad!" said Lachlan absently. "How are you coming along with your sales percentage?"

"I'm about two-thirds of the way there," said Jimmy.

"Well, what do you say I let you have it for that, then?"

"And I'd be through working then? I could go back to my parents?"

"That's right."

"No way," said Jimmy, turning back to the rack of clan ties.

"A-weel . . ." Lachlan straightened up suddenly. "Jimmy, why don't you slip round to the refreshment tent and get us a shandy, if they have any left?"

Jimmy took money and hurried off through the crowd, wondering vaguely if Lachlan's ESP was troubling him again. He glanced back and saw the old man talking to a blonde in an oriental outfit. He would have given a lot to know what clan Lachlan would contrive for *that*.

"Good morning, ladies and gentlemen, and welcome to the Glencoe Mountain Highland Games herding competition . . ." Over the scratchy loudspeaker, it sounded like *hernia composition*. Three black and white border collies were crouched at the sidelines beside their respective owners waiting for the signal to begin. The announcer explained that because of space limitations and—he paused—other considerations ("Sheep shit," said Geoffrey), the dogs would be herding ducks instead of sheep. "Our first contestant is a five-year-old border collie, Somerled of Skye Laird, owned and trained by Marjorie Carter Hutcheson. Somerled won the competition last year."

"Isn't he beautiful?" said Elizabeth. "I remember when he was just a puppy."

"By the pricking of my thumbs . . ." muttered Geoffrey as Marge approached the wooden duck box.

The three of them were sitting with a group of pipers in full costume. The piping events were next on the program, and the young men had brought their instruments and a deck of cards to while away the time before their performance. Cameron was watching the card game with a studied air of nonchalance, but he kept glancing nervously at the field.

"This is a wonderful event," Elizabeth prattled on. "Would you like me to explain it to you?" She waved encouragingly to Marge and Somerled.

"I would thou couldst," Geoffrey intoned.

Elizabeth frowned. "Are you barding again?"

On the field, the dog was wriggling with anticipation as the door to the box swung open. Five white ducks waddled out uncertainly into the sunlight and began to wander off in five different directions. Somerled, whose first job was to march the feathered troops through a concrete pipe, crouched before one duck, intending to drive it back into the group. Unfortunately for the veteran collie, it was a rookie duck. Instead of trotting back to the platoon, it emitted a honk of outrage and flapped its wings. This gave Somerled pause: in his experience, ducks never argued back. He lunged at the left flank of the rest of the group, attempting to steer them toward the pipe. More honking and flapping.

"That's odd," said Elizabeth. "I wonder what's the matter with the ducks."

One of them had broken away from the group and was making a determined rush toward the crowd. Somerled abandoned the rest and gave chase, trying to circle in front of the deserter. Marge's look of astonishment had turned to anger, and she was conferring with the competition judge, who kept shrugging and shaking his head.

"Good gracious!" said Elizabeth. "You'd think those ducks had never seen a dog before!"

"Bring me no more reports; let them fly all!" moaned Geoffrey.

Cameron, who had once played Malcolm in the sixth form, replied, *"I'll to England."*

Geoffrey threw him a look of gratitude. *"To Ireland, I."* He nodded, getting to his feet. *"Our separated fortune shall keep us both the safer."*

"What is the matter with you two?" demanded Elizabeth. "Oh, dear, look at that duck!"

Standing up was Geoffrey's chief mistake: Marge recognized him. She made it to the edge of the crowd almost as fast as the duck had, and pointed accusingly at Geoffrey. "You! I saw you messing with that herding box yesterday! What is wrong with those ducks?"

In considerably less than Shakespearean tones, Geoffrey told her; but Walter Hutcheson, who had been watching from the other side of the field, had not stayed to see the confrontation. He had seen the fiasco made of Somerled's herding efforts, and immediately suspected sabotage. Several bystanders distinctly heard him say "Colin Campbell!" before he stalked away.

Afterward, everyone agreed that things could have been much worse. Geoffrey hadn't been seriously injured, and the piper found, after playing a few trial notes, that his bagpipe hadn't been damaged at all.

. . .

Andy Carson looked at his watch for the third time in as many minutes. The parade of the clans should have started ten minutes ago, even allowing for the usual tardiness. He wondered if he should go ahead and start his speech and let the stragglers catch up. Still, he didn't like to begin with a clan chief missing. It was hot, though; and Scotch and Gatorade had turned out not to be such a brilliant idea after all.

"Is Ramsay here yet?" he asked Margaret McLeod.

"Yes, he just arrived. Everyone has signaled ready except the Campbells."

Andy shrugged. Normally, Colin Campbell was the first one on the field and the most vociferous complainer about latecomers.

"Shall I go and get him?" asked Margaret, consulting her clipboard.

"I suppose. I'll do my introductory speech while you're gone. Just do hurry him up, will you?"

Elizabeth, who had changed back to her kilt for the ceremony, was present but not yet in place. "This won't take long," she promised Cameron. "You have to be wearing the clan colors to participate, though, so I'm afraid you'll have to watch it from here. Hold Cluny's leash, will you, while I tie his tartan ribbon?"

Cameron took hold of the leash and looked around at the mass of people crowding the field. He didn't see any signs of weapons, though. "Just what is going to happen now?" he asked uneasily.

"The parade of clans. The master of ceremonies will make his speech, and introduce guests, and then each clan will march out on to the field, shout its battle cry, and stand off to the side until all the clans have been presented."

"And then what?" No cannons, either.

Elizabeth smiled. "Then I change back into my sundress, and you take me to lunch."

"Right. How's Geoffrey?"

"He stayed at the cabin with a washcloth across his forehead, doing the death scene from *Hamlet*."

"As whom?"

"Oh, everyone. Geoffrey feels that death is too important to be enacted only once." She took back Cluny's leash. "Time to join the clan. I'll be back as soon as I can."

Margaret McLeod clasped her clipboard protectively to her chest. Rousing the Campbell boar from his lair was not her idea of a pleasant morning's work, and she wished she had thought to tell someone to go and get the blasted chief, but there was no time for that now. She could already hear Dr. Carson's nasal tones droning over the loudspeaker.

Another disagreeable thought occurred to her. Suppose Campbell was drunk. He would hardly be alone in experiencing that condition, she thought ruefully, but it might make it difficult to get him to the ceremony. She should have brought help, she thought, looking up at the camper door. Oh, well . . . She tapped gently. "Dr. Campbell? It's late! The ceremony has begun!"

Nothing.

"Dr. Campbell! Are you in there?" Margaret tried the door handle, hoping that she was *not* about to find out what Colin wore under his kilt.

The door swung open, and she found herself face-to-face

with the clan chief himself. "You're late!" Margaret cried, before she got a good look at him and discovered that he was indeed the late Colin Campbell.

CHAPTER NINE

The forest clearing had that strained sound of great activity striving for silence: the scrape of boot leather against brush; the faint click of metal; and through it all the rhythmic current of breathing. Gray-clad bodies, blending like shadows into the broom-sedge, edged up the hill with their Enfield rifles, slowly and silently creeping toward the boulder at the summit. A pebble dislodged by a boot heel made scarcely as much noise as a sweatbee hovering overhead.

Behind the troops, a hawk-faced man with silver sideburns and officer's braid sat astride a bay mare, his hand upraised to signal the charge.

Everything was as still as a Matthew Brady photograph of Shiloh: Confederate troops prepare to advance! The soldiers looked back for the go-ahead, but it was forestalled by a spell-breaking sound from the colonel's belt. Brrrh! Brrrh!

Alexander "Lightfoot" MacDonald's voice shattered the stillness. "Stop the goddamn war! I got to answer the phone!"

Margaret McLeod had had the presence of mind not to scream. A nurse for several years before she married Peter, she knew how to handle death scenes. Quickly verifying her first impression that Colin was indeed dead, she hurried back to the grandstand where Andy Carson was continuing to delay the ceremony by prolonging his opening remarks. The wool-clad troops, many of whom had been toasting each other's health all morning, were growing restive.

Margaret caught Andy's eye, and motioned for him to let someone else take the podium for a while.

"What is it?" he hissed. "I was just coming to the punch line!"

Seeing his face drain of color when she told him, Margaret concluded that her punch line had been better than his. "What should we do?" he whispered, casting an anxious glance at the field full of suspects.

Margaret had already thought this out. "You go up and announce the coming events for the rest of the day, and read the names of the competition winners if you have to. I'll go to the rescue-squad truck and get them to radio the sheriff."

Andy Carson looked down at his sheaf of notes, and back at the sweaty crowd on the field. "How long will it take him to get here?" he whined.

The sheriff was on the scene in less than ten minutes, but this was ninety per cent luck and only ten per cent departmental efficiency. When the squad radioed in about a possible homicide at the Scottish festival, dispatcher Charlotte Revis weighed the two relevant facts in the matter: that it was Sheriff MacDonald's day off, and that he was actually in Glencoe Park, within a mile or so of the death scene. Ranking business before pleasure, Charlotte put through a call on the sheriff's mobile telephone to relay the message.

"Damnit, Charlotte, what is it?" rasped the sheriff's voice

in her ear. Beep!

"Where are you, sir?"

"Fighting the Battle of Wicker's Ford Hollow! Over!"

Lightfoot MacDonald was the colonel of the local Civil War reenactment militia, and as Charlotte knew, the troops were having a dress rehearsal for next Saturday's mock battle in Glencoe Park. If she knew her park geography, the battle site should put the sheriff within a mile of the Scottish festival.

"We have a ten thirty-three out where you are. Can you ten twenty-one, please?"

Another beep. "I rode the horse over behind some trees, so I can talk now. What is the nature of the ten thirty-three?" He listened, dodging tree branches while Sorrel switched and stamped at botflies. "Right," he said at last. "I'll go over there now. Put in a ten seventy-nine to meet me there, please. Out."

Lightfoot MacDonald stopped long enough to turn over his command of the rehearsal to Wilburn Blevins, saying only that he had "police business," and then he cantered Sorrel up the nature trail toward the Glencoe meadow.

Andy Carson mopped his forehead and ventured a smile at the glowering crowd in front of him. "I apologize for the delay," he said again. "But it shouldn't be much . . ." His voice trailed away into an open-mouthed stare.

Coming toward him from a break in the pines was a Confederate army officer on a large brown horse. The apparition, complete with sword and canteen, trotted across the field, skirting clumps of clansmen, and stopped beside the speakers' platform.

"I'm Sheriff Lightfoot MacDonald," said the soldier. "I'm here in response to a call you people put in for assistance."

"Yes. Mrs. McLeod can show you where he—the—it is. Can I go on with the ceremony?" The natives looked not only restive but, in some cases, a few over the limit, as well.

Lightfoot shrugged. "Sure. As long as nobody gets in my way. You might ask anyone with information to come forward." He leaned back on his horse to wait for the announcement.

Dr. Carson wandered back to the podium. "Fellow Scots," he began. He wondered who had snickered when he said that. "It is my sad duty to announce to you that the presentation of the clans has been delayed because of the untimely passing of the chief of Clan Campbell, and we have reason to suspect foul play."

Lightfoot MacDonald looked up sharply at this; but before he could interrupt, a wobbly fellow in a blue kilt shouted, "This is Glencoe! It's the MacDonalds who got murdered, isn't it?"

"We're paying them back!" shouted a wag from the MacDonald ranks, waving his hip flash. *"Return to Glencoe!"*

"Hell, you didn't do it!" roared a Murray, not to be outdone in the joke. "The Murrays owe the bastards for Culloden!"

"Up the Stewarts! Up the Stewarts!" chanted a red-kilted bunch in center field.

Someone else countered with, "Down with Campbells!"

Andy Carson looked helplessly at the grim-faced sheriff.

"What's going on here?" hissed the sheriff.

Carson sighed. "They think it's a joke, I'm afraid. Because he's a Campbell."

Lightfoot shook his head. "I'll talk to you later," he said, turning his horse. "I'd like to see the body now."

"Of *course* I didn't touch anything," said Margaret McLeod in her calm, efficient voice. "I could see that he was dead. I used to be a nurse."

Lightfoot grunted. "We'll go over the place when my deputy gets here. Did you notice the cause of death at the time?"

Margaret nodded. "I could see the blade sticking out of his chest, and of course I recognized it." Seeing his look of surprise, she hastened to add, "I don't mean that I know who it belongs to. I mean that I knew what it was."

"A dagger."

"No. A *skian dubh*. Well, I guess it is a dagger, but it's the one that men wear in their kilt hose when they're in Highland dress."

The sheriff thought back to the crowd assembled in front of the speakers' platform. "You mean all those jokers were armed?"

"Most of them," Margaret admitted, though she wouldn't have thought of it that way herself. She looked pointedly at Lightfoot's cavalry sword.

"Now, just what had this man done to make all those people hate him so much?"

Margaret McLeod hesitated. "You mean personally or . . . otherwise?"

The sheriff blinked. "There's an otherwise?"

"Oh, yes. He was a Campbell, you see."

"So who would want to kill a Campbell?"

"Why, everybody."

Half an hour later, the site examination was well in hand, and the sheriff was able to turn things over to the deputy and the coroner, and to proceed with the questioning of witnesses. He had taken over the hospitality tent as a makeshift headquarters—with Sorrel tied to one of the support posts.

"Now, let me get this straight," he said to the still-fidgeting Andy Carson. "You people are all mad at this fellow over something that happened in 1746?"

Andy searched for common ground. "Well, Sheriff," he said brightly, "it was *their* Civil War."

"Uh-huh," said Lightfoot. "But *we're* not still stabbing people."

"We're not, either, that I know of," said Dr. Carson mildly. "But I did announce your request for information, and there are a few people who came forward and asked to speak with you."

Lightfoot relaxed. This case might not be such a blister, after all. With a good six hours of daylight left, he might make it back to the war. He enjoyed an occasional outing with the local militia—it gave him a sense of history and a form of recreation that seemed less dandified than golf. Also, it met his need for an element of drama. Most people might assume that sheriffing would supply all the theatrics one might require in life, but that was an outsider's view of the job.

To Lightfoot's mind, being a peace officer was a lot like fishing: ninety per cent psychology and patience, and only ten per cent confrontation. Most of the drama associated with the office of sheriff lay in public appearances: cutting an imposing figure at the county fair, making the occasional speech to a civic group, and generally personifying the law, with a pearl-handled pistol and a shiny brass badge. Lightfoot was good at it. He had the foxlike Cherokee-Scots bone structure to look the part, but he couldn't call the work exciting, this case included. Likely as not, some drunk would turn out to have done it without meaning to, and the whole sorry mess could be dumped in some lawyer's lap by morning.

He looked at his notes on the case. The deceased had been an M.D., aged sixty-three; that he had been in fine health was the only good word anybody had to say about him so far. In Lightfoot's experience, cantankerous old men got themselves avoided, not murdered; he wondered what the wrinkle was in this case.

"Who's first?" he asked Andy Carson.

Jerry Buchanan, still colorful in his clan tartan, came forward. "I am, sir." He gave his name, being careful to add that he was a dentist, because the very dullness of his profession added to his credibility.

"And what information do you have about the deceased?" asked Lightfoot politely.

"It was a political killing!" hissed Jerry. "He was assassinated by the S.R.A.!"

Lightfoot looked up. "Spell that."

"It's like the I.R.A.," Jerry explained. "The Scottish Republican Army. They're planning to pull out of Great Britain, just as America did in 1776."

"And Dr. Campbell was a member?"

"No, of course not." Jerry Buchanan began to look uncomfortable. Maybe it wasn't such a good idea to appear too knowledgeable about terrorist activities. He certainly hadn't bargained for *domestic* killings when he'd joined the Cause. Car bombings in Edinburgh were all very well, but dammit, this was Virginia! "Look, Sheriff," he said in an undertone, "I think the person you should really be discussing this with is the British secret agent here at the games. He's probably conducting an investigation of his own."

"How do you know there's an agent at the games?" asked Lightfoot reasonably. He didn't have to deal with too many crackpots in Clay County, but he'd heard that big-city police were ankle-deep in them.

"He's MI5," Jerry muttered. "I heard one of the terrorists mention him. And I just saw him a few minutes ago on the practice field." He gave a brief, but very accurate, description of Cameron Dawson.

"The sheriff wants to see me?" asked Cameron, glancing at Elizabeth. "What about?"

Andy Carson sighed. "About the murder investigation, I presume." He wanted to ask Cameron about his alibi for last night, but he thought it best not to get involved. "Would you like me to phone the British embassy?"

"I think I can manage this one on my own, thanks," said Cameron. He looked at Elizabeth. "Do you suppose they'd let you come along?"

"I doubt if it's very important," said Elizabeth. "You didn't know Colin Campbell, did you?"

"Yes, he did," Dr. Carson put in. "Met him yesterday."

"Damn!" said Cameron, pronouncing the word as if *Notre* came before it. "The bloke who was on about sea monsters!"

He walked to the hospitality tent, framing a careful explanation of his slight acquaintance with the deceased and trying to decide how best to express a correct, but detached, sense of regret at the gentleman's passing. He was, therefore, completely unprepared for the sheriff's line of questioning.

"Am I a *what?*"

"Whatever you English call them." Lightfoot shrugged.

"I'm not English. I'm a Scot," snapped Cameron. He would answer to British or Scottish, but *not* English, and certainly not Scotch.

"You seem familiar enough with English, though," the sheriff observed. "However, if you need an interpreter, we can see about finding you one."

Cameron closed his eyes. What did they bloody think he spoke? "Just ask your questions, please. Or better yet, tell me what this is about."

Lightfoot MacDonald flipped again through Cameron's passport, looking for some indication of his status with the government—a telltale 007 stamped beside his name, for example. He said carefully, "According to my information, Mr. Dawson—"

"*Dr.* Dawson."

"Whatever. According to my information, this was a political killing, and as an agent for the English government—"

"British!" muttered Cameron under his breath.

"You would have some knowledge of the circumstances."

"Right. This dotty old man who had a thing about sea monsters gets killed with a *skian dubh,* and you think the British government is responsible?"

"No, sir. According to my information, the Scottish Republican Army killed him."

Cameron stared. "Nonsense! You have us mixed up with Ireland. There is no Republican Army in Scotland. And I am not a secret agent for anybody! I'm a marine biologist. I do *seals* and *porpoises.*"

"Do you know the Earl of Strathclyde?"

"I'm practically sure there isn't one. I mean, I haven't got Debrett memorized, but I've certainly never heard of an Earl of Strathclyde."

"One . . ." Lightfoot consulted his notes. "Geoffrey Chandler."

"Ah," said Cameron, with an arctic light in his eyes. "Now we're getting somewhere."

"I've sent someone to fetch Mr. Chandler," said Andy Carson. "Meanwhile, Sheriff, perhaps you'd like to interview somebody else. I promised her I'd mention it to you."

"Why waste time?" Lightfoot shrugged. "I'll talk to everybody, and sort it all out later."

"Are you sure you want me to stay, Sheriff?" asked Cameron.

The sheriff nodded. "If you are a secret agent, you certainly can't admit it. Everybody knows that. And even if you aren't, why, you might be helpful to me in the investigation, because I don't know much about this Scotch business."

Cameron cringed. *Scotch.* But there might be a diplomatic limit to the number of times one should correct a policeman, so he said nothing. He didn't think he was going to be much help, though.

The next witness was a sturdy little woman in her mid-forties, dressed in what Lightfoot considered the preppy golfing costume: tan canvas skirt, knit shirt, green espadrilles. Only the tartan scarf pinned to her shoulder indicated that she was a festival participant.

"Hello, Sheriff," she said in her board-of-directors voice. "I'm Lacy Campbell."

"Any relation to the deceased?" asked the sheriff, making a note of the name.

Lacy Campbell stopped, open-mouthed. Was this a trick question? "Well," she said, "I suppose back in Argyll, if you assume that the Ian Campbell of Glenlyon was the same Ian Campbell who in 1787—"

"So you weren't his wife or his daughter or anything?" the sheriff put in.

She smiled. "Oh, no. In the sense you mean, we weren't connected at all. He was just the president of our clan society, and of course quite a lot of us are named Campbell."

"How come you're not wearing a kilt?"

"Oh, Colin Campbell would have had a conniption, Sheriff. It is not traditional for women to wear kilts, and no matter what the other clans do, Colin was not about to permit it in ours."

The sheriff looked at Cameron for confirmation, and received a barely perceptible nod in return.

"Now, as to what I wanted to report in connection with Colin's murder"—Lacy Campbell permitted herself the briefest of smiles—"I suppose you think it odd that I should be so composed—and, really, it has been quite a shock hearing about the poor man; but to tell you the truth, he wasn't as popular as he might have been. Several people dropped out of the group altogether because Colin was such an overbearing old . . . Anyway, he had arguments with everybody, but I did happen to know of one quite recent one that might be important."

"Not the sea monsters!" cried Cameron. Seeing the others' look of astonishment, he scrunched down in his seat. "Sorry," he murmured. "Carry on."

"We'll get to that one directly," Lightfoot promised him. "Now, what were you referring to, ma'am?"

"The first part I only heard about, but I witnessed the second one. Have you heard of Dr. Walter Hutcheson? No? He's the president of the MacDonalds this year, and he and Colin are both physicians at the community hospital. Myra Logan told me that she heard Colin and Walter Hutcheson arguing yesterday. Myra's girl is in the country-dancing competition with my Fiona. Myra said that they were actually shouting—something about real estate, she thought. Well, I didn't think too much of it at the time, because somebody is always shouting at Colin Campbell, but then today at the herding fiasco—"

"Fiasco?"

Lacy Campbell digressed to explain about the mysterious appearance of rookie ducks in the herding box, and the resulting chaos. "I was standing right beside Walter Hutcheson watching the whole thing, and I distinctly heard him say 'Colin Campbell' as he stalked off looking like thunder. Now, the reason I think that's important is that the exhibitor in the sheep trials was Walter's wife. Well, his ex-wife, actually, but they're still friends, I believe. They'd been married for *decades,* you know."

"So you think he might have killed Colin Campbell over some ducks?" asked the sheriff carefully.

"No. But I think he might have gone to argue with him about it, and one thing may have led to another," said Lacy Campbell, proud of her powers of detection.

Lightfoot MacDonald considered it. "Cantankerous old body, wasn't he?" he mused. "So he put rookie ducks in the dog trials?"

"No, he didn't!" Cameron blurted out. "We did. The Earl of Strathclyde and I."

After collecting a few more particulars about her testimony, the sheriff shooed Lacy Campbell politely out of the tent and took a long look at the uncomfortable Cameron Dawson. He flipped again through the blue British passport, reading the visa, the description, and making a face at the passport picture.

"You've been here . . . I make it three days."

"Just about," Cameron agreed.

"Uh-huh. Three days. And you've already made contact with a terrorist organization, had an argument about sea monsters with a man who promptly gets murdered, and now you tell me you're responsible for this herding duck business?"

Cameron sighed. He didn't believe it, either. In Scotland he'd been pretty average, studied a lot—the word *dull* came to mind. It's the American insanity, he thought ruefully; I'm infected already.

"Haven't established a time of death yet, but suppose you tell me where you've been for the past twelve hours or so."

"Since midnight? Well, last night I went to the Hill-Sing with a girl and a bobcat, and—this morning about eight, I—"

"Whoa! Back up. I ain't even going to *speculate* about the bobcat, but are you telling me in an understated English way that you spent the night with her?"

One did not, Cameron presumed, lie to law-enforcement persons. "Yes."

Lightfoot gave him a look of open admiration. "Boy, you limey spies are something else, man! And I thought James Bond was all hogwash! You are something else!"

CHAPTER TEN

Marge Hutcheson sat in the refreshment tent, brooding over a cup of coffee and an ashtray full of cigarettes. Across the table, Elizabeth tapped her can of Irn Bru and looked again toward the hospitality tent.

"He's been in there a long time," she murmured.

Marge smiled briefly. "Stop being such a mother hen. He's fine. I'm sure the sheriff has sense enough to realize that no one who just arrived in this country could have anything to do with all this."

"I guess not."

"Poor Colin."

Elizabeth frowned. She had been shocked that anyone should be murdered at a Highland festival, but his being Colin Campbell was not particularly surprising. She wondered what to say to Marge without having to lie about her own reaction to the death. "Did you know him well?" she finally asked.

"Oh, the way people do. We've all belonged to the Scottish society for donkey's years, and I never found Colin particularly hard to get along with. I think he was lonely, but he couldn't be bothered with meek or unintelligent people." Marge grinned. "Fortunately, I am neither."

"I wonder why he was killed?"

"I wonder if we'll ever know. So many crimes seem to go unsolved these days. And this certainly can't be the sort of case or the class of people that the sheriff is used to dealing with."

Elizabeth looked thoughtful. "Maybe he needs some help," she murmured.

"I suppose it would be useful to know whom Colin annoyed in the past two days," Marge remarked. "There's your cousin Geoffrey with that Carson man. Now if *he* ever gets murdered, you can put me down as chief suspect."

Elizabeth shook her head. "There's a waiting list of people wanting to kill Geoffrey," she sighed. "But I am sorry about the dog trials."

"It is kind of you to take an interest in this, Sheriff," said Geoffrey Chandler grandly, before anyone could speak. "However, I do not wish to press charges against my assailant. *What's done is done and cannot be undone.*"

The sheriff looked at Cameron for clarification. "The bagpipe," said Cameron. "You remember. This is His Lordship, the Earl."

Geoffrey frowned. More improvisational theatre, he thought. "Is this not about my little contretemps this morning?" he purred.

"No, sir, this is a murder investigation, which we believe

to be connected with terrorist activities. I understand that your code name is Earl of Strathclyde?"

Geoffrey sank into the nearest folding chair. "I think perhaps that my injuries may have been more severe than I thought," he murmured. "But do carry on. I shall be fine."

"Tell us what you know about the Scotch Republican Army," said Lightfoot grimly.

It was too much for Cameron. "Scottish!" he said. "Scottish! *Scottish!* Not Scotch. Scotch is a drink."

"The Scottish Republican Army, then," said Lightfoot MacDonald. "I thought you said there wasn't one, Dawson."

"No, but if there were, it would be Scottish, not Scotch."

"There isn't one?" asked Geoffrey brightly. "Are you certain?"

Cameron hesitated. "There may be some group of loonies somewhere who play at it, but as a serious political organization in Scotland—no, definitely not."

Geoffrey grinned. "Brilliant! It's foolproof."

"What is?"

"The plot of *Macbeth* . . . the cathedral at Rheims . . . guacamole dip. What was that, Sheriff?"

"You're talking rubbish," Cameron told him.

"Sorry . . . Must be that head injury kicking in again. I think I should go and lie down, don't you?" He stood up. "Let's do this again soon, Sheriff, shall we?"

"Count on it," growled Lightfoot.

"Do you need any help getting back to the cabin?" asked Cameron. He knew a performance when he saw one, but he wanted to talk to Geoffrey alone.

"Siddown, Scotty," the sheriff snapped. "We're not through yet."

A man in a brown uniform appeared at the entrance to the tent. "Got the reports for you, Lightfoot!" he announced.

The sheriff looked from the suspects to his deputy. Geoffrey, seeing his hesitation, pitched against a table. "*Dark Victory* . . ." he intoned.

"I'll come straight back," Cameron promised, helping Geoffrey up.

"Ten minutes," growled the sheriff. He watched the two of them stumble away in a grade-B performance of the walking wounded. He didn't think Geoffrey's information would be relevant to the case, but he might follow up on it anyway, just to see what was going on. "Assholes!" he grumbled.

The clan tents and the festival meadow had vanished around the last bend in the trail. "Are you going to cut it out now?" Cameron demanded. "I'm letting go."

Geoffrey straightened up. "I nominate you for best supporting actor," he said generously. "Not bad for a novice."

"Right. Now what the fuck are you up to?"

"Oh, do they have that word in Scotland? How interesting!"

"We have a lot of words you might be familiar with. Mayhem . . . kidney punch . . . disfiguration . . ."

Geoffrey shuddered. "I'll bet you paint yourself blue when you're angry."

"*One* of us will be blue," Cameron assured him. "Now, look, Geoffrey, come off it. That Campbell guy is really dead, and the sheriff has got some daft idea that I'm a spy, and I get the feeling that you're up to your neck in all of it. Now, I know you're Elizabeth's cousin, and I don't want to get you in trouble, but I'm going to find out what's going on."

"I was going to tell you," Geoffrey said with a pout. "Seeing as how we're duck-brothers. I just didn't want to reveal anything in front of the sheriff, because Lachlan is such a decent old man and really, those clowns deserve it."

"Lachlan Forsyth—the souvenir man?"

"Yeah. And the head of the S.R.A."

They were passing a wooden picnic table tucked away in a small clearing, and Geoffrey motioned for Cameron to sit down. "It's very simple, really. The old guy noticed how Irish Americans were so hot to support the I.R.A., and he figured that the Scots, who have even more money, ought to be just as eager to kick in a few bucks for a cause. We're very big on causes over here."

Cameron nodded. "It's quite shocking. We drove past a bank yesterday, and a big sign in the window said, OPEN AN I.R.A. ACCOUNT WITH US TODAY. I couldn't believe it."

Geoffrey sighed. "No, idiot. That's an Individual Retirement Account. I'd explain it to you, but it's boring. Anyway, the plan was absolutely foolproof. He gets these clowns to give him money to support a secret terrorist organization in Scotland, right?"

"Okay. What does he do with the money?"

"He keeps it! That's the beauty of things. They feel all noble and committed, and nobody gets hurt."

"But what happens when they notice that things aren't getting blown up in Glasgow?"

"Hasn't anything happened in Scotland over the past

year? Shipwreck? Train wreck? Bridge collapse?"

"Nope."

"Well, if it had, he'd have claimed credit for it, I bet. And if nothing did happen, he'd just say that they weren't ready to make their move yet, and he'd advise them to be patient for a while longer. Better yet, he'd hit them up for another donation."

"Surely somebody would get suspicious sooner or later."

"Yeah, I guess so. But what could they do about it? Can't you picture somebody going to the FBI and saying: 'Excuse me; I contributed money to a terrorist organization, but they haven't killed anybody yet.' You may not be aware of it, but it's illegal to support that kind of thing. They'd be in a lot of trouble. No, it's foolproof. Once they gave him money, he had them like crabs in a barrel."

"I suppose so," Cameron agreed. "But it's dishonest. He's a con man, you know. Why didn't you want to turn him in?"

"Oh, out of sheer admiration, I guess." Geoffrey shrugged. "What an actor to pull off a scam like that. And he's a nice old boy, really. Didn't you ever know that somebody was putting on a colossal bit of phoniness, but you didn't have the heart to turn them in?"

Cameron nodded. "Yes," he said slowly. "I guess I have felt exactly like that."

Lightfoot MacDonald glowered at his deputy. "I have had a bellyful of foolishness," he warned. "I hope you're not going to try to sell me on suicide, or some such tomfool notion."

Merle Fentress shook his head. "Not me, Sheriff. It was

homicide. Regular old stabbing, excepting for the fancy knife they done it with. It nicked the lung and punctured the heart. Pretty near instantaneous, we reckon."

"Time of death?"

"Early this morning. Seven or eight, the coroner thinks."

"Got the site done?"

"Yep. Photographs and all."

Lightfoot grunted. "No fingerprints, of course?"

"Oh, yes, sir. Prettiest little set of prints you ever seen on that knife hilt."

Lightfoot grinned. "Got your print kit in the trunk?"

"You bet. I'll get it now." As Merle headed out to the patrol car, he could hear Sheriff MacDonald whistling "Just Before the Battle, Mother." It was a good sign.

Cluny was sleeping in a wicker dog basket beside the Chattan information table while Elizabeth stapled together more clan brochures. She didn't want to find Cameron just then, because she wanted to think about Cameron—not an easy thing to do when he was around.

She ought to be checking on Colin Campbell's activities over the past two days, but it was difficult to take much of an interest in it. Interest. *Inn*-terrrest, she thought, trying to remember how he would pronounce it. It didn't come out right, somehow. She hadn't heard him talk long enough to be able to play it back in her head. Such a pretty accent. She wondered if the magic ever wore off. If, after years of hearing it, someone said to you: "Where's the bloody sports page?" or "Slow down before you kill us," would it still sound gentler and more significant than hearing it in American dialect?

"Snap out of it!" she said aloud. "Your brain is turning to haggis!"

She looked up to find Heather McSkye Hutcheson standing on the other side of the table, leafing through a brochure.

"Hello," stammered Elizabeth, hoping she hadn't been overheard.

Heather, who was now more conventionally dressed in a pink shorts outfit, smiled at her. "Where's the Sloane Ranger?"

"Cameron? He's around somewhere." Elizabeth wondered how helpful she ought to be, and what a Sloane Ranger was, but Heather wasn't the sort of person she wanted to get chummy with. Really, Marge was much easier to talk to. Men had no taste, she decided.

"Yes, well, it was nice meeting you at the party and all. Did . . . Cameron . . . say aught about it?"

Elizabeth wondered what she meant by that. "Not really," she said in a puzzled voice. "Why? Did you two know each other back in Scotland?"

Heather laughed at the note of anxiety in Elizabeth's voice. "I wouldn't mention it to him if I were you."

Change the subject, thought Elizabeth. I don't even want to think about this. What else can we talk about? Oh, yes! "Isn't it shocking about Colin Campbell's being murdered?" she said brightly, relieved at having found a safer topic.

Heather shrugged. "I thought murder was pretty routine over here."

"Not as casual as all that. Did you meet Dr. Campbell?"

"No, I don't think so."

"Yes, of course you did! I saw him going up to you at the party just as we were leaving. Did he say anything significant to you?"

"I don't remember him. I met so many people last night."

Betty Carson, who had been getting ice out of the cooler, turned around. "Colin Campbell, Mrs. Hutcheson? He was that short little man with white hair who asked you about your new cousin—the Duke's child. I was standing right behind you."

"Oh, yes. Him."

"And he asked you something about its layette, didn't he? I thought I heard him say baby sham, or pillow, or something."

"Did he seem upset about anything?" asked Elizabeth.

"I didn't notice."

"Yes, he must have been," Betty put in. "Because later Walter told my husband Andy that there would be a committee meeting this morning. Colin Campbell had some bee in his bonnet about embezzlement, or some such thing. Didn't Walter mention it to you?"

"He may have done. I wasn't paying any attention. Goodbye." Heather walked away, obviously annoyed at the continual interruptions from Betty Carson.

Elizabeth made a mental note to file *baby sham* and *embezzlement* away for further consideration, but her chief concern was the relationship between Cameron and Heather. Just how well did they know each other, and did it matter? Of course it's none of my business, Elizabeth told herself, so I'll have to be very subtle indeed when I check up on it. She stapled the rest of the pamphlets to the tune of "You Ain't Woman Enough to Take My Man," but a small, cold part of her mind refused to believe the lyrics.

She was still stapling ten minutes later when the deputy told her that the sheriff wanted to see her.

Alexander Lightfoot MacDonald wrinkled his nose at the smell of booze in the tent. He didn't mind a cool brew with the militia boys, but sometimes the smell of it took him back. Six years old . . . with the Stars and Bars tacked over his bed . . . and Daddy stumbling in to bid his little corporal good night, reeking of bourbon and Sen-Sen. Little Ellick, as they called him then, would edge away from the fumes and stare at the sepia picture of Stonewall Jackson on the dresser, while Daddy told him war stories.

He must have been twelve before he knew that Guadal-canal wasn't in the War Between the States, but by then it was too late to take an interest in Daddy's war—or in Daddy, who finally finished the Japs' job for them by wrapping himself around a tree in his black Bel-Air. Lightfoot wasn't there at the time, but since then he'd pulled enough drunks out of wrecks piece by piece to have remarkably realistic nightmares about it.

Now Lightfoot was the county sheriff—maybe a little rougher on drunk drivers than he needed to be—and people laughed at the way he played war with the young bucks of the county; but to Lightfoot's mind, it was a better way out of this world than most of the other exits he'd seen people try.

He took a swig of hot, un-spiked Pepsi, and picked up his notes on the Campbell case. Glencoe Park was private property, so the alcohol was not his concern—not until one of them tried to turn one of his county roads into the abattoir. Then he'd see. Meanwhile, he had to try to make sense of this three-ring circus: Scotchmen, spies, an old man hellbent on cussedness. . . . Seemed like none of it was really serious. All these people were on French leave from their real lives, he reckoned. In costumes up on a mountain, they just didn't seem to *count* things up here as part of real life—just part of the show, as if they expected the dead man to come back to life on Sunday afternoon, the way the casualties did in his Civil War battles.

He shrugged. Why not? Most of them weren't involved, and not one gave a rat's ass about the deceased. But somebody at this sideshow was playing for keeps, and in an encampment full of play-acting simpletons, that could be godawful dangerous.

"'Scuse me, Sheriff. The young lady's here," said Merle, who had started to knock on the tent flap.

"Right. Bring her in."

She looked about twenty-three, and a little like Linda Ronstadt on one of those early album covers, Lightfoot decided. Didn't look as though she could put a knife into hot butter, much less an old man, but you never could tell. Stabbing didn't take much effort at all if the blade was sharp, and that one had been.

"Have you got her fingerprints?" he asked Merle.

"Yessir. We're pretty near through with that. Got most everybody that we know of who had a connection with him."

Elizabeth rubbed her smudgy fingers with a tissue. *"Out, damned spot! Out, I say!"* Geoffrey's form of insanity was highly contagious, she thought sadly. Lightfoot took her name and address, and spent several minutes trying to make sense of the Maid of the Cat concept. He finally decided that it was something like the Carolina ram that was paraded at UNC football games, and he let it go at that.

"I understand you had a run-in with the deceased yesterday," he remarked.

"Well, he fussed at me for wearing a kilt, and I told him what I thought of him. But neither of us took it as a capital offense."

"How well did you know Dr. Campbell?"

Elizabeth considered it. "If somebody in your neighborhood kept a vicious dog in a fenced-in yard . . . about as well as you'd know the dog."

Lightfoot laughed. "Mainly by reputation."

"Exactly. There may not be people around with better motives for doing him in, but I bet there are a lot of people with similar ones."

"Quite a few," the sheriff admitted. "We got one woman that he reduced to tears by telling her what he thought of the tartan she was wearing."

"The Royal Stewart, I'll bet. Nobody's entitled to wear it, really, but Dr. Campbell was the only person who'd pitch a fit."

"Can you think of anyone who had better reasons to want him dead?"

"No. No one ever bothered to stay around him long enough to . . . wait a minute. He did have one friend. Marge Hutcheson. I'll bet she could tell you what he was really like."

The sheriff made a note of the name. "One more thing. Do you know anything about a terrorist organization connected with the games?"

Elizabeth shook her head. "It sounds unlikely. Is it something to do with Scotland? You might ask Cameron—"

"Cameron Dawson?"

"Yes. But I doubt if he'll know anything at all about the games. He's just arrived in this country, you see, and for most of that time . . ." She blushed.

Lightfoot looked at her closely. "Oh," he grunted. "So you're the one."

Elizabeth smiled sadly. "Sheriff, I devoutly hope so."

Of all the people Lightfoot had seen so far, Marge Hutcheson looked the most upset. She had not been crying, he decided, but she appeared to be under a strain. He offered her his empty Pepsi can for an ashtray, and watched her light a Benson & Hedges with shaking hands.

"How well did you know the deceased?"

"Well enough to mind that he got himself murdered," said Marge grimly. "Poor Colin. I expect he would have enjoyed all the fuss. He was much more comfortable with dissension than he was with friendliness. He was always trying to drag me into an argument."

"About what?"

Marge smiled. "The weather . . . the stock market . . . anything at all. It was a bit of a game with him, you know. He didn't take quarreling personally, so I don't think it would occur to him that people might actually get their feelings hurt in an argument."

"You think he pushed somebody too far?"

"Perhaps. I used to tell him he would someday. But I never pictured any consequences more serious than a

126

punch in the nose."

"Did he mention any specific run-ins he'd had with anyone lately?"

"Little things. He had a quarrel with the Maid of the Cat because she was wearing a kilt. Nothing important."

"Ummm." Lightfoot glanced at his notes. "There was an argument that seems a little more serious than that. With a Walter Hutcheson. Your husband?"

"Ex-husband," said Marge, stubbing out her cigarette.

"Colin Campbell was heard to threaten Dr. Hutcheson with . . . something about zoning rights to lakefront property. Would you know anything about that?"

Marge smiled. "More than Walter does, I expect. I'm the one who decided that we should buy the land. We wanted to build resort homes and condominiums at the lake—to develop the area into a major vacation area."

"How could Campbell affect those plans?"

"Well, the other major property holder on the lake is the university, and Colin was a trustee. I expect he told Walter that he'd get the lake declared off limits to construction. Make it a game preserve, perhaps."

"How much money are we talking about here?"

"The original investment? Three hundred and sixty-seven thousand dollars."

Lightfoot whistled. "I'd say that argument beats out the quibbling over costumes."

"Oh, but he was bluffing, Sheriff. He was only one trustee, and by no means a popular one with the rest of the board. Surely you don't think he could have persuaded them to rezone the lake to accommodate his personal vendetta?"

"For that amount of money, I can see how someone might not be willing to risk it. Is your ex-husband a violent man, Mrs. Hutcheson?"

"No, of course not. Walter wouldn't even fox-hunt."

"What kind of doctor is he?"

Marge looked uncomfortable. "Well, he's a thoracic surgeon, actually."

"I see," said Lightfoot, looking pleased. "And did he have a skiing . . . a skein . . . one of those daggers?"

"You'll have to ask his wife," said Marge coolly. "I know that he used to have two of them, one for day and one for formal wear, but since one of them was a gift from me—"

"What did it look like?"

"Sterling silver hilt . . . stag's head on top. It was for our silver anniversary."

"Knives are unlucky presents," said Lightfoot without thinking.

"So it seems, Sheriff."

"I might want you to take a look at a dagger later. Could you identify the one you gave your husband?"

"I suppose so."

"Well, I guess that's all the help I need right now. This business sure has taken some figuring out, though."

"What, the Highland games?"

"Yep. A whole lot of customs that I'm not at all familiar with. Of course, my people were Scotch."

"MacDonald. Yes."

"In fact, I'm right proud of the one that came over from Scotland. He was a soldier in the Revolutionary War. Wrong side, damn him. But still a soldier."

"Oh, really? A Tory, was he?"

"Yep. I'm named after him, too. Alexander MacDonald, and he was captured at the Battle of Moore's Creek, outside of Wilmington, North Carolina."

Marge stared at him. "Good God! Moore's Creek! Do you know who he was?"

"Sure, he was a Tory soldier, about twenty-five—"

"He was the son of Alan and Flora MacDonald from the Isle of Skye! They emigrated back to Scotland after the battle. *Sheriff, you are descended from Flora MacDonald!*"

Lightfoot blinked. "Who's she?"

After the brief flurry of excitement over the murder and its aftermath of law-enforcement people, the games had settled back into the usual ritual. The country dancing competition proceeded smoothly from the *Ghillie Callum* to the *Shean Triubhas* to the accompaniment of recorded bagpipe music; and on the main field, an assortment of kilted linebackers gathered to begin the serious athletic competition.

"In the two-hundred-twenty-one-pound hammer toss . . ." bawled the loudspeaker.

"Here you are!" said Geoffrey, spotting Elizabeth near a dancing platform. "I've been looking all over for you."

Elizabeth scowled. "I thought you were dying."

"Well, one thought of remaining discreetly closeted in one's room for dramatic effect, but then one remembered that one had signed up for the saber toss, and decided to make the most of one's fleeting existence. You are going to watch, aren't you?"

"Oh, yes, I certainly am," said Elizabeth with a curious smile. "It will make my day. Is Cameron with you, by the way?"

"He may have been looking for you, too. Where were you?"

"Talking to the sheriff. He wanted to know about the tête-à-tête I had with Colin Campbell."

"Any clues yet?"

"I don't know. He asked me about terrorist organizations. What do you suppose that means?"

Geoffrey shrugged. "I think it's a wild-goose chase. I certainly don't believe that Lachlan . . . maybe I'd better go over to the group now."

"Are you sure they'll let you? Oh, never mind." Elizabeth smiled at her cousin. "What is it they say in the theatre? Break a leg?"

"You don't have to say it so *sincerely*," Geoffrey complained. "Well, I'm off. Cameron should turn up soon. He seemed pretty anxious to see this event, too."

He ambled toward the recorder's table to check in for the event. When he was safely out of earshot, Elizabeth began to giggle.

"Sixty-eight feet, four inches!" cried the announcer as the measuring official signaled the results of the last hammer throw.

"Has it started yet?" asked a voice behind her.

Had Elizabeth been as good at barding as Geoffrey was, the appropriate response would have been: *My ears have not yet drunk a hundred words of that tongue's utterance, yet I know the sound. Art thou not Romeo* . . . As it was, she managed the proper surge of adrenaline, if not the lines, and slipped her hand into his. "Has what started yet?" she murmured.

"Geoffrey's saber toss. You didn't tell him, did you?"

"Of course not! I was afraid *you* might."

Elizabeth turned back to watch the hammer-throwing competition, but her mind had settled on Heather; and she was busy turning words inside out in her head, trying to find a connection between Heather and Cameron, based on something they'd said. They had used a lot of unfamiliar words, though, and she couldn't remember any. Jimmy and Senga . . . pet names for each other . . . that was a bad sign. But what was that other odd phrase, something to do with carpeting, she had thought at the time. Of course!

"Cameron, what does *shag* mean?"

"What? Who said it?"

"Oh, I don't know . . . I heard it somewhere."

"You've not only heard it, you've done it as well."

Elizabeth gasped. They had been discussing . . . *that?* She let go of Cameron's hand. "I saw Heather today," she said in a shaky attempt at casualness.

"That was a good throw! Did you see that short bloke? I think he's won it." Cameron appeared to take a great interest in the competition.

"I guess she was pretty surprised to see you," she said carefully. She had decided to assume that he and Heather knew each other before, and see if Cameron corrected her.

"I think we have things straight between us," Cameron murmured.

Elizabeth wanted to shut her eyes. "Were you surprised that she's married?"

"A little. I'm certainly not going to interfere, though. Ah! Look what's coming up now."

The loudspeaker crackled again. "The caber toss, as you all know, lads and lassies . . ." Cameron winced. ". . . consists of tossing one of these eighteen-foot poles so that it makes a perfect rotation and lands with the thin side up. The cabers weigh about a hundred and twenty pounds apiece, so you can imagine the strength required to turn them end over end . . ."

"Did Geoffrey really think they were going to throw *swords?*"

"Sabers, yes. Until a second ago, he didn't know a caber from a hole in the ground. Where is he, anyway?"

"Slinking away past one of the dancing platforms. I wonder if they'll call his name out?"

"I know just how he feels," sighed Elizabeth.

Walter Hutcheson thought of law-enforcement officers chiefly in terms of traffic control, and since this was a murder investigation he was somewhat at a loss on how to proceed. He finally decided to look solemn and concerned in his best civic-meeting attitude, and to try to appear as objective as possible. Something in the sheriff's manner made him uneasy.

"You knew Dr. Campbell pretty well, didn't you?"

"Over twenty years at the hospital." *For my sins,* thought Walter.

"Good friends?"

"Good professional relationship as colleagues."

"Any idea who would want to kill him?"

"Everybody!" snapped Walter Hutcheson. "The man couldn't walk down a hallway without stirring up an incident. His personnel folder read like a synopsis of World War Two. The question is: who finally lost control and killed him?"

"It might depend on the size of the argument, don't you think?"

"I suppose so, but Colin could be aggravating about practically anything."

"Real estate, for example?"

Walter flushed. He might have known that somebody would get wind of that, considering how loudly Campbell had been shouting when they discussed it. "Colin Campbell was a bully, Sheriff," he said at last.

"Maybe so. But even bullies follow up on threats now and then. He doesn't sound like the sort of person that I'd want to bet big money on. Why don't you tell me your side of it?"

Walter explained about the lake property and Colin's threat about rezoning, and about the hospital hearing inquiring into Dr. Campbell's conduct. The sheriff listened carefully, making an occasional squiggle on his yellow notepad. He seemed to be listening only out of politeness, as if he were waiting for something. Walter found out what it was a few minutes later when the deputy appeared holding something wrapped in a towel. Lightfoot accepted the package, and squinted up at Fentress.

"Anything for sure?"

Merle Fentress glanced at Dr. Hutcheson. "I'd say so. Go on ahead." He leaned against one of the tent supports, shook the canvas a little, and straightened up again, trying to stay deadpan.

Lightfoot ignored him. Pulling the towel away from the package, he held out a *skian dubh* sheathed in a plastic evidence bag. "Do you recognize this, Dr. Hutcheson?"

"It looks like mine," said Walter, before the obvious implication of its appearance struck him. He hastened to add, "There must be hundreds of identical ones."

"Did you bring yours to the festival?"

"Yes, of course. I wear the silver one for evening dress."

"Perhaps we might go along to your camper and see if you can locate yours, doctor."

"I suppose someone might have stolen mine," said Walter as an afterthought.

"Uh-huh. Well, this particular one has your fingerprints on the hilt. And we found it sticking in Colin Campbell's chest."

"This must be some kind of appalling mistake, Sheriff."

"Why don't we go back to your camper, sir, and check for your dagger. It won't be necessary to handcuff you, will it? Of course, if you can't produce yours, I'm going to have to read you your rights and ask you to come with us."

Walter Hutcheson staggered out of the hospitality tent, trying to make sense of the last ten minutes, but it was like trying to read a newspaper in a windstorm: his thoughts would not stay still long enough for him to examine them.

He knew, really, without going back to the camper, that the *skian dubh* was his. There was a little nick on the stag's nose from when he'd dropped it accidentally. His indecision was halfway between hope and playing for time while he tried to figure out what was happening. Walter's head hurt; it was unfair to expect acute thinking when he'd been celebrating for most of the past twenty-four hours. Colin Campbell couldn't even die without inconveniencing everybody.

As they walked along the path encircling the festival field, Walter spotted a familiar face and stopped in his tracks. "Marge!" he cried. "The most dreadful thing has happened! Colin has got himself murdered with a *skian dubh* that looks like mine, and I may actually be hauled off by the police. We have to straighten this out."

Marge looked at him gravely. "I'm sorry, Walter."

"Well, of course you are. It's unthinkable, isn't it? Now, I want you to call Sanderson and tell him to drive down here, because I may need a lawyer. Just as a precaution. And . . . let's see . . . maybe you ought to get hold of Dr. Fahrner in case I'm not back by Monday . . ."

Instead of springing into brisk efficiency as Marge usually did, and adding to the list of things to be done, she was just standing there, expressionless. What's the matter with her? Walter wondered. "Now, let's see . . . Sanderson, Fahrner . . . is there anyone—"

"Don't you think your wife should be doing this?" asked Marge quietly.

"What?"

"I said: don't you think your *wife* should be doing all this?"

Walter felt like a dog who had reached the end of his chain at a dead run. Heather. He had forgotten all about her. "Yes, of course," he murmured. "I can't tell you how sorry I am—"

"I know," said Marge.

CHAPTER ELEVEN

Lachlan Forsyth, three-deep in babbling tourists, wondered for the fourth time where Jimmy had got to. When the lad's parents had insisted on taking him to lunch—reeking guilt, he thought smugly—he had assumed they were going to haul him off for a nosh at the refreshment tent; but apparently their relief at having disposed of him was so great that only The Thistle Inn and a couple of London broils could deaden it. He didn't know whom he felt the most sorry for—those two yuppie simpletons who wanted a Cabbage Patch doll that breathed, or little lizard-hearted Jimmy who was meant to be an Artful Dodger. No use giving either party advice, though. Might as well try to tell chalk how to be cheese.

The McGowans had tried to seem pleased at how hard their Jimmy was working at the festival, but behind the smiles they were wondering what the trick was to managing him—and feeling the reproach that they couldn't do it themselves. None of his business, Lachlan told himself. Just be glad for a bit of help at the festival, when you had so much unexpected bother to see about.

"Do you have any books about Clan Graham?" asked an elderly woman in a ridiculous-looking tam.

"No, but they'll be in that big book along with the rest of them."

"But I'm only interested in Grahams."

"Leave your name, then, and I'll see if I can special order for you. Who was next, please?"

The stall work was so routine, and the questions so repetitious, that it hardly took any concentration. Lachlan wrapped packages and juggled credit cards while he considered the murder. It was almost funny that someone had killed Campbell, but for the inconvenience of it in terms of his own plans. He really couldn't afford to have police officers nosing around the games. As it was, he was dreading the inevitable interrogation scene. He supposed that sooner or later they would get around to questioning him. In a fish-bowl like this, he had to assume that someone had over-heard his quarrel with Colin Campbell.

Well, he had planned for that contingency. He would thicken his burr to the consistency of creamed cheese, and vow that he had nae idea whatsoever what these blood-thirsty Americans could be getting up to in the name of clan rivalry. He considered claiming kinship with the Campbells on his mother's side, but that might leak out, and it would be bad for business.

Lachlan picked up his half-full can of shandy—it was closer to the woolens than he was used to putting it. This murder business was making him absentminded, he thought. Waving time-out to his customers, Lachlan took a swig of his drink, making his usual silent toast, the Cultoquhey litany: *From the greed of the Campbells, From the ire of the Drummonds, From the pride of the Grahams, From the wind of the Murrays, Good Lord, deliver us.*

James Stuart McGowan turned up a few minutes later, looking less bored than usual. He elbowed his way past the browsers. "Sorry I'm late!" he called to Lachlan. "Something interesting happened!"

"Oh, aye? Got your dad to give you power of attorney, did ye?"

Jimmy grinned. "Nah! Nothing interesting ever happens with *them.* I did shake them up a bit when I ordered a shandy with lunch. I would have gotten away with it if the waiter hadn't asked, 'I suppose you want it without the beer, young man.' "

Lachlan shook his head. "They'll no be pleased, Jimmy."

"When we were coming back into the festival, though, guess what we saw? The sheriff arresting somebody!"

Lachlan looked wary. "Oh, aye?"

"Yep. He didn't have on handcuffs, but they put him in the backseat of the squad car, where there aren't any door handles. He had changed back into regular clothes to go to jail, but my dad recognized him anyway."

"Arrested? For the murder, do you mean?"

"Of course. You wouldn't do drug busts on an affluent crowd like this," said Jimmy smugly. "Don't you want to know who the collar was? Take a guess—I mean, with your ESP."

"For killing a Campbell?" Lachlan took a deep breath. "Would it by any chance be the president of the Mac-Donald clan?"

Jimmy grinned. "You got it! Walter Hutcheson. What do you think of that?"

"It grieves me," said Lachlan Forsyth. "I was hoping to stay out of it."

"Of course, he's a well-known surgeon, so he probably has a competent attorney on retainer, don't you think? He'll probably make bail on his standing in the community and be out of the slammer by six o'clock."

"What did you say, laddie?" murmured Lachlan. "I was thinking about something else."

In hushed and well-bred tones, the word spread quickly around the festival that Walter Hutcheson had been taken in for questioning in connection with Colin's murder. Elizabeth, on duty at the Chattan tent, heard it from Betty Carson, who maintained that Walter had been acting strangely for some time now, and she wondered if he might be taking narcotics.

"I wonder how Marge is taking this," Elizabeth said to Cameron.

"Is that his former wife?"

"Yes. Oh, I see what you mean. But Cameron, they were married for ages, and Marge isn't the sort of person who holds grudges. Why, I'll bet she'll even be speaking to Geoffrey again in a year or two. I think I should go and see how she's doing. Will you watch Cluny for me?"

"I'm not even in Highland dress," Cameron protested. "Why should I have to mind him?"

Elizabeth smiled. "Because you have a Ph.D. in biology, sir—I'll be back soon!"

She hurried down the path toward the practice meadow, and Cameron scratched Cluny's ears and watched her go. "I only do seals and porpoises," he said with a sigh of resignation.

Somerled, the border collie, was on his chain in front of Marge's tent, so Elizabeth knew that she had come to the right place. Marge was there. She wasn't sure exactly what tone to adopt about this recent development, but perhaps she could take her cue from Marge's behavior. If nothing else, Elizabeth could run errands or offer to look after Somerled.

"Hello," she said softly, peering into the tent. "What a reek of smoke!" she added, leaning back and coughing. "If you're going to chain-smoke, you ought to do it out in the open where there's oxygen to compensate."

Marge did not look up. "I don't know what to do," she said.

Elizabeth ventured in, fanning the air in front of her. "About Walter, you mean?"

"Yes. It's all so complicated."

"What does he want you to do?"

In a halting voice, Marge told her about their encounter just before the arrest, and Walter's list of instructions. "He had forgotten all about her," said Marge. "Anyone could see that. And I don't know what to do."

"I think you should do what's best for Walter," said Elizabeth, who felt that that was both a comforting and a neutral thing to say.

Marge nodded and reached for the pack of cigarettes. "Yes. Perhaps I should." After a few moments' silence, she remarked, "Walter didn't kill Colin, you know."

Elizabeth shook her head. "I don't know anything about it. I'd heard they had a fight."

"Yes, but I have known Walter for most of his life, and I assure you that he is not a murderer."

"Well, I suppose they might let you testify as a character witness," said Elizabeth kindly. She felt that such testimonials would be ridiculous as well as useless, but she meant to be soothing until Marge could get a grip on herself.

"He did not do it."

"Then I'm sure that the sheriff's investigations will turn up something in his favor, and everything will be all right."

"I wouldn't count on that," said Marge grimly. "They have that stupid real estate argument as motive, and they asked me about Walter's *skian dubh,* so presumably that was the murder weapon. And I know they fingerprinted a bunch of us. The fact that they took Walter away must mean that they found his prints on it."

"That's a pretty strong case," Elizabeth admitted. "Maybe Walter has changed. I mean, he has been doing some strange things in the past few years, hasn't he?"

"You mean Heather?"

"Well . . . maybe he's going through some mid-life crisis, and—"

"Walter's beyond mid-life crisis," snorted Marge. "He now qualifies as an old fool. But I don't think he could change enough to start stabbing people."

Elizabeth was beginning to feel restless. *There's no reasoning with her,* she thought. *Women in love have one-track minds. I wonder what Cameron is doing?*

"What the sheriff needs is some new evidence. He won't be looking for any more himself. He thinks he's solved the case." Marge sighed. "Of course, no one would believe me. I'm not objective. I doubt if anyone would tell me anything anyway."

Elizabeth's heart sank. "I suppose that I could sort of ask around and see if I can come up with anything in Walter's favor."

"Colin must have quarreled with lots of people at the festival," Marge mused.

"He had run-ins with Cameron and me, but we didn't do it."

"Yes, but besides that."

Elizabeth thought about it. People had been discussing the case around her all afternoon, and occasional remarks had filtered through her thoughts about Cameron. She tried to remember what some of them were. "Betty Carson said something about Dr. Campbell wanting to call a committee meeting this morning."

"Oh? That could be important! Colin would only do that if he intended to launch a large-scale donnybrook. I wonder what he was up to?"

"Something about embezzlement, I thought."

"Money? Nonsense. The committee has accountants coming out of their ears, and half of them are lawyers anyway. Are you sure she said embezzlement? It doesn't matter. It was probably third hand anyway. Who would Betty have heard all this from?"

"Dr. Carson, I imagine. He's on the committee."

"Good. Talk to him."

Elizabeth sighed. "I wish I could talk to Colin."

"Yes, that would solve everything, wouldn't it?"

"Not about the murder. I was just thinking. Betty said that Dr. Campbell seemed to know a lot about Heather's background. They were talking about a new baby in the family."

"Heather's background?"

Elizabeth nodded miserably. "I think she and Cameron knew each other back in Scotland. I'll bet Dr. Campbell could have told me what was going on."

"I'll bet he would've, too," said Marge grimly. "That's the trait that killed him."

Walter Hutcheson's present wife was sitting alone in the camper, trying to decide what to do. Walter had shouted a lot of instructions at her as they were leading him away, something about telephoning a lot of people. But he hadn't left her any phone numbers, and the address book was back at the house. She supposed she could leave the festival and drive home. She'd never driven the camper, though, and it would be like maneuvering a great bloody aircraft carrier on the two-lane roads. She might get herself killed.

Heather had not been crying, but she was tense and afraid. What if things didn't turn out all right? Sod the stupid police anyway for arresting Walter. She looked at the half-empty bottle of Glenlivet in front of her. Better not have another—not that she was too keen on the taste of the stuff anyway. This was not a time to be losing control. The police would be back along asking questions of her, she was sure. When did you last see your husband's *skian dubh?* What time did he leave the camper? Was there any blood about him?

Heather twisted a strand of hair and tried to decide if she ought to do anything. Walter would call his own lawyer from the police station, wouldn't he? And like as not, they'd arrange the bail, and then he could come and drive her home. She didn't like to ask anyone for help just now; she wanted to be alone. It would all work out, she thought. It had to. Cameron Dawson reminded her of why she had left Scotland, and why she didn't want to go back. Americans—and Walter in particular—were a bit simple, but she was enjoying herself, and she wasn't going to see it spoiled. Cameron Dawson . . . In spite of her worries, Heather giggled remembering the look on the little brunette's face when they'd talked about him. . . . Silly git.

She wondered what Walter's former wife was doing. She was the Maggie Thatcher type, all right. If it had been her here as the defendant's wife, she'd have already called the President and organized a league of Friends of Walter Hutcheson. A geriatric Girl Guide was Marge.

She started at the sound of the knock on the camper door.

Not the bloody cops already! Heather opened the door cautiously, ready to slam it if she caught sight of a camera. "Oh," she said. "It's you, Jimmy. If you don't give me any of that Your Ladyship rubbish, you can come in."

Questioning people at the Highland games wasn't going to be as easy as Marge seemed to think. Elizabeth knew that elderly Virginians were the last people in the world to take a young girl seriously—and if they did, they would resent her. She had wasted a good bit of her social life having to be wide-eyed and respectful while pompous old bores held forth on their pet subjects. The liberal-arts types were the worst. They always managed to steer the conversation to the inch-wide sea of whatever their specialty was and to dismiss anything else as not worth knowing. That's why I fall for scientists, Elizabeth thought: I give them credit for being brilliant because they can do things that I can't—and they're not given to talking about it over dinner.

She had been unable to find Andy Carson to ask him about Dr. Campbell's proposed committee meeting, but another member of the group, Hughie MacDuffie, was all too evident. Elizabeth hesitated. Was she really desperate enough to commit herself to a conversation with Mac-Duffie? Conversation was hardly the word for it, though: a few utterances of "Oh, really?" were the most that Hughie would permit in the way of participation in his monologue. He taught ancient history at a military academy, and was given to telling jokes with the punch line in Latin.

I might as well get it over with, thought Elizabeth, gritting her teeth. "Hello, Dr. MacDuffie, how nice to see you!" she said aloud.

Hughie MacDuffie's victim, who had been subjected to a lecture on Tacitus's opinion of the Scots, took advantage of the momentary distraction and fled. The professor looked over his black-rimmed glasses at Elizabeth, either trying to place her or mentally flipping through his list of conversational harangues.

"MacPherson, isn't it?" he said, eyeing her sash.

"Yes, sir. Maid of the Cat this year." I may as well volunteer it, she thought; we're not going to get anywhere until I do. "My parents are Douglas and Margaret MacPherson, and my older brother Bill is a law student."

"Any kin to David MacPherson of the Upperville Hunt Club?"

"No. My mother is one of the North Georgia Chandlers. Timber."

"Ah! Splendid weather we're having for the festival, isn't it?"

Elizabeth sighed. It was a science, after all, communicating with this bunch. Seals and porpoises couldn't be any trickier. She spent another few minutes making the correct noises before launching her chosen topic of conversation.

"Isn't it shocking about poor Dr. Campbell?"

"Abiit ad plures," said Hughie solemnly.

"I'm sure he'll be greatly missed. Such a busy man! You were on the committee with him, weren't you?"

"I like to think that, like the second Triumvirate . . ."

Elizabeth ignored the gambit. If I let him get started on Rome, we'll be here for days, she thought. "Had you talked to Dr. Campbell lately?" she asked.

Hughie MacDuffie cocked his head, trying to recall the faces of his conversational victims. "Colin Campbell . . .

yes . . . because I remember saying to him: *tantum religio potuit. . . .*"

"What was he talking about?"

"Campbell? He wanted to get the committee together this morning. He didn't though. Never turned up."

"He was dead," Elizabeth reminded him. "Now, did he say what the meeting was about?"

"Fraud. I remember, because I said—"

"Fraud? You're sure it wasn't embezzlement."

"No, my dear. The two things can be very different. For example, when the fire department of Rome was run by—"

"Did he say who the fraud concerned?"

"Oh, someone here at the games, I believe. Something about . . . what did he tell me? . . . I'm afraid I wasn't listening as attentively as I might—Colin was such an old bore. Of course, had I known that he would be killed, I would certainly have paid attention. I think a dentist was asking him about tartan patterns. But that doesn't make sense, does it? Unless it's like the Oracle of Delphi. Have you heard the story about the fellow who went to the Oracle. . . . Let's see, it was . . ."

There was no formal registration for the Highland games. People paid their admission at the gate without signing anything. New members could, if they wished, put themselves on a mailing list at one of the clan tents, but even then occupation was not listed on the form. Anyway, with more than fifty clan tents, it would take days to track down the information, with very little chance of finding the right one. How do you find a dentist in a haystack, Elizabeth wondered. The only solution that occurred to her was more drastic than she cared to undertake. Clearly, it was a job for Geoffrey.

She found him in the Keith tent, sharing a bottle of Dewars and the plot of *Brigadoon* with two of the clan officers.

"And then he goes back to New York, right? So . . ."

"Geoffrey!"

"Hello, Elizabeth. How odd to find you Scot-free. As I was saying—"

"Geoffrey, I have a part for you in a small drama."

Geoffrey, noting her serious expression, set down his plastic cup with a sigh of regret. "Once more unto the breach, dear friends . . ."

When she had steered him out of earshot of the Keith contingent, she said, "I suppose you want to know what this is all about."

"I'll tell you what it had better not be about," said Geoffrey menacingly. "If you have had some kind of altercation with your Highland laddie and are expecting me to play Friar Laurence in any way whatsoever . . ."

"It isn't that. I have to find a dentist."

Geoffrey raised his eyebrows. "Wouldn't it be easier to ask Cameron his age? You could sneak a look at his passport."

"Shut up. This has nothing to do with Cameron. I've been looking into the business about Dr. Campbell, and it turns out that he wanted to call a committee meeting this morning because of some fraud connected with the games. One of the committee members says that he found out about the fraud from a dentist."

"*Why* are you playing sleuth, dear cousin? Shouldn't you

be at the library checking out books on seals and porpoises?"

Elizabeth blushed. "I don't know what you're talking about. Anyway, the sheriff has arrested Dr. Hutcheson, and he didn't do it, so I'm going to try to uncover some new evidence."

"How do you know he didn't do it?"

"Marge is convinced of it. She's such a saint. You wouldn't catch me being that worried about a man who had left me for someone else."

"No, my dear. Beneath your little pixie face lies the soul of Clytemnestra." Seeing her look of bewilderment, he explained, "Wife of Agamemnon. When her husband came home from the Trojan War with a pretty little captive, she took a knife to both of them."

Elizabeth thought about Heather, but her better nature refused even to consider the fantasy. "I don't need another classics lesson," she snapped, remembering Hughie MacDuffie. "I'm doing my good deed by trying to clear Walter Hutcheson—if he is innocent. And my only lead so far is the dentist who talked to Colin Campbell about fraud."

"You want me to help you find a dentist?"

"Exactly."

"How, pray?"

Elizabeth told him, steadfastly ignoring his look of increasing reluctance.

Several minutes later, the games announcer was drawn away from the microphone by his assistant. "An emergency, Grace?"

"Yes. Look at this poor boy."

Geoffrey, who had invoked his look of suffering from *The Spanish Tragedy*, cringed beside her, holding a handkerchief to his cheek. "Impacted what'sit," he murmured, swaying a bit.

The announcer's eyes strayed back to the playing field. If he lost his place now, it might take the rest of the afternoon to get things straight again. "Oh, really?" he murmured, edging away.

"Dentist!" wailed Geoffrey.

The assistant announcer gave his arm a motherly pat. "There, there, you poor thing. Ray, couldn't you just make a quick request for a dentist to report to the control booth?"

Ray hesitated. "Couldn't somebody drive him to town?"

"Weekend . . ." whimpered Geoffrey.

Ray scowled. It was going to be easier to make the announcement than to argue with a tottering invalid. "Right," he said. "Go and sit down over there, and I'll see what I can do."

Geoffrey crept over to a folding chair near the announcer's table to await further developments. After a minute or two Elizabeth slid into the empty chair beside him. "Good work!" she whispered. "You must have been very convincing!"

"Yes. I hope you're equally persuasive when the tooth fairies arrive, so that they don't remove my jaw in an excess of Samaritanism."

"I just hope I can figure out which one I need to question."

"I think you ought to stick to less complicated good deeds in the future," Geoffrey remarked.

Elizabeth nodded. It wasn't entirely an act of charity,

though. If she could clear Walter Hutcheson of the murder charge, then Heather would still be a safely married woman, and then whatever there was between her and Cameron wouldn't matter. Would it?

Ten minutes later, only one person responded to the broadcast appeal—a diffident young man in a blazing yellow and orange tartan. "I don't carry any tools with me," he explained. "But I thought I'd just come along and offer advice, if you needed any."

"Thank you very much for coming," said Elizabeth politely. "Actually, I needed to ask you a few questions about the murder."

He gasped. "I've already spoken to the sheriff." Noticing Geoffrey for the first time, he began to back away. "It was a trap, wasn't it?" he hissed. "I didn't mean to tell them, sir . . ."

Geoffrey lowered his handkerchief and glared at the cowering dentist. "You would do well to give this young lady all your cooperation," he said sternly. "She is an operative."

"Who is this?" muttered Elizabeth.

"I'm Jerry Buchanan, ma'am. And I just wanted another tartan!"

Tartan! Elizabeth nodded grimly. "And you discussed this with Colin Campbell, didn't you?"

"Well . . . yes. I know he wasn't one of us, but I knew that he was an expert on Scottish tartans and things, and I didn't think it would do any harm to ask."

"What did he say?"

"Well, I asked him who assigned tartans to the different clans, and how you got in touch with them, and he wanted to know why I was asking." Jerry glanced about nervously. "At first I refused to tell him, but then when I asked if an earl had the power to change his clan's tartan, he started to browbeat me, and I guess I let some information slip about the S.R.A."

Elizabeth, who was mystified, was about to ask what the S.R.A. was, but Geoffrey interrupted her, "The organization was news to him, of course?"

"He was furious about it. Wanted to know who was behind it."

"And you told him . . . ?"

"I didn't mention you!" Jerry protested. "Honest! Well, I'd forgotten your name, actually."

"So you told him about Lachlan," said Geoffrey smoothly.

"I may have mentioned him."

Geoffrey stood up with the dignity of an irate prince. "We will take no action against you," he said grandly. "But your earldom is canceled."

Jerry Buchanan nodded miserably. "Just don't kill me."

"Out of my sight!" thundered Geoffrey. He kept up the pose of outrage until the yellow and orange tartan had disappeared into the crowd on the sidelines.

"What the devil is going on?" Elizabeth demanded. "And why do *you* know anything about it?" she added as an afterthought.

"Oh, that. I told you that it was handy to know Shakespeare. Apparently, I stumbled on to the password of a terrorist organization."

"Terrorists? You mean *they* killed Dr. Campbell?"

"No. They don't kill anybody, dear. They just think they

do." He explained to Elizabeth about Lachlan Forsyth's scheme for profiting from the misplaced patriotism of the more radical Scottish-Americans. "He told me all about it after I crashed the conspirators' party. He really didn't feel too bad about taking their money. The way he figured it, he was keeping them from doing real harm with their money, and he provided them with a little excitement. It was very theatrical, really."

"You have the morals of a fungus!" Elizabeth informed him. "I suppose you wouldn't have dreamed of reporting this to the sheriff?"

"I didn't feel that it was relevant. Lachlan is a con man, not a killer."

"Ha! Does Cameron know about this?"

"I told him a little while ago. That worm of a dentist may have forgotten my name when he was talking to Colin Campbell, but he dropped it in front of the sheriff quick enough. They hauled me in for questioning this morning as a high-ranking official in the S.R.A."

"What about Cameron?"

"Well, that may have been my fault. In an excess of youthful spirits last night . . ."

"Drambuie!"

"Precisely. As I say, in an excess of good spirits, I told the conspirators that Dr. Dawson was a British secret agent."

"Oh, my God. Geoffrey, somebody is going around *killing* people at this festival! How do you know you didn't put Cameron in danger?"

"Your concern for the prince of pancake syrup is most touching, but there is something in your indifference toward my well-being that I don't quite like."

"You could be wrong, you know. Lachlan Forsyth may have killed Dr. Campbell in an attempt to cover up his illegal activities. Is he a U.S. citizen, do you think? If convicted of a crime, he could have been deported."

"Back to Scotland—the air fares to which you were lamenting at the National Trust booth earlier? Oh, worst of fates!"

"Hush. Be serious for a minute. He may not have wanted to go back to Scotland. Maybe he's wanted for being a con man there."

"Really clever people do not kill their enemies. They outwit them. My faith in Lachlan is unshakable. You, on the other hand . . ."

"I'm going to talk to Lachlan Forsyth. Now that we know what the fraud was. . . . Say, how did Colin Campbell know that the organization *was* a fraud?"

"Common sense!"

"Not entirely. Knowing what an old bully Campbell was, I'll bet you anything he had it out with Lachlan last night."

"Perhaps."

"I'll talk to him first. Then I'll check for witnesses to that quarrel."

"Go to, then. Have you no further need of a Watson? I thought I might go and observe the country dancing. For purposes of choreography."

"Fine. If you see Cameron, tell him I'll find him later."

"Perhaps you'd like to compose a singing telegram?"

Elizabeth, at a loss for a clever rejoinder, made a face at him and hurried away.

The pageantry of the festival hardly registered with

Elizabeth now. Her mind was too busy with shades of gray. Did Lachlan Forsyth kill Dr. Campbell in order to protect his con operation? Did one of the conspirators do it out of misplaced patriotism? Or, in the heat of a quarrel, did Walter Hutcheson do it after all? What's Heather to him or he to Heather?

The meadow was getting hot again as the mid-afternoon sun bled the color out of the landscape. Elizabeth was glad that she had given up wearing her tartan; it was really too hot. Besides, she wasn't sure anymore what it meant. In all the previous festivals, it had meant: I am Scottish; this is the badge of my culture.

But the one thing Cameron did—besides make her heart turn over when she looked at him—was to make her uneasy about the significance of that culture. Every time she knew some bit of Scottish history or tradition and Cameron did *not* know it, it made her wonder just what they were preserving so carefully with their little groups. Perhaps it was culture of a sort, but it wasn't Scotland. Elizabeth, who had been a sociology major, considered the disparity. What did it remind her of? A culture artificially preserved like . . . Latin. The language so carefully nurtured in the Vatican was a piece of culture preserved like a fly in amber; but modern Italian was a living culture, Latin that had been allowed to evolve. One was dead and the other was alive. Less colorful, maybe (how would Cameron look in a kilt?), but still alive, the real thing.

She decided that she wasn't surprised about Lachlan Forsyth's con game. She remembered how the festival folk had spoken approvingly of his being a *real* Scot. He wore the kilt, spoke some Gaelic, and knew all about the plaids and the history. He was, in fact, a professional Scot. Now that she had Cameron to compare him with, it was obvious to her that Lachlan was up to something. He was too good to be true.

He wasn't there.

The canopied souvenir stall was as busy as ever, with tourists two-deep at the record bins and pawing through the woolens, but the only person behind the counter was a little blond boy. Elizabeth's purpose wavered as she looked at the wonderful bits of bric-a-brac at the stall: thistle-patterned china, toy Nessies, a case of jewelry. Maybe she should get Cameron a MacPherson scarf: he ought to know his own tartan. . . . She waited patiently in the same spot for several minutes until the boy behind the counter had time to notice her.

"Where is Mr. Forsyth?" she called out.

James Stuart McGowan shrugged. "I don't know. He said he was taking a break, but it's been over an hour. Can I help you?"

"I just need to talk to him. Can you tell me which way he went?"

He nodded toward the crowd encircling the stall. "My visibility isn't too great here. He lives in a silver AirStream, though, and it's parked in the campsite." He looked at her closely. "You were here before, weren't you? Talking to him about which hand to eat with, or something?"

"Yes," said Elizabeth, deciding not to correct his version of the conversation.

"I thought so. Right after you left, he wrote something down on a piece of paper, and he said he'd give it to you if you came back. Let's see . . . where'd he put it?" He looked up at her slyly. "Of course, I should be spending my time attending to real customers."

She sighed. "Give me a scarf in the MacPherson tartan."

"Hunting or dress?"

"Dress. Now find me that paper."

"Here it is. He wrote it on this paper bag. Just the right size to put the scarf in. Will that be cash or charge?"

When Elizabeth had completed her purchase, she walked away from the crowd and examined the four words scrawled across the paper bag. She smiled. He really was a sweet old man. And as for the message . . . she hoped that she would have the occasion to use it.

Lachlan Forsyth's AirStream trailer was easy to find. Its windows bore stickers of the Scottish lion, the flag of Scotland, and one bore the legend *Ecosse*—French for Scotland. On its bumper was the usual assortment of Highland games bumper stickers. Elizabeth wondered if he lived in the contraption year-round, or if he had some other home during the winter months. Surely he couldn't spend his whole life going from one festival to another? Technically, of course, he could: in the Sun Belt states, festivals went on right through the winter months. It seemed like an empty sort of life, though. What could be fun and exciting for a weekend might be a form of insanity if one tried to live it on a regular basis.

Elizabeth shuddered. To spend one's life in a kilt, rehashing long-forgotten battles . . . Was Lachlan taking a detour around the twentieth century or was he planning to amass an S.R.A. fortune and leave Brigadoon far behind? Impossible to tell. No one really *knew* Lachlan Forsyth.

His kindness and his comic-book Scottishness would keep you enchanted until he went away; and when the spell wore off, you realized that you didn't know the first thing about him.

Elizabeth knocked on the trailer door.

No answer.

After a few minutes of impatient waiting, she knocked again, louder this time. But there were no sounds from within, and no sign of life. Sign of life? Elizabeth tried the door handle. It was securely locked. Even in *Brigadoon*, the threat of twentieth-century vandalism pervaded one's consciousness, she supposed.

By standing tiptoe on the top step and leaning over to the left as far as she could, she could just manage to get a grip on the tiny metal windowsill and peer inside. No one was there. And no body, she thought to herself with a sigh of relief. Now, where else could he be?

Elizabeth decided to check the clan tents in case Lachlan had gone visiting. Maybe she'd even find him at the MacPherson tent: he had seemed to enjoy talking to Cameron. Strangers in a strange land, and all that. As she walked past the rows of campers, she saw the MacDonald banner flying in front of one of the campers. The Hutchesons. Heather. Might he be visiting Heather? She was another Scot, after all. Surely someone as steeped in history as Lachlan Forsyth would relish the chance to talk with the niece of a duke.

Perhaps she ought to stop in and see Heather, anyway. Elizabeth could not believe that the new wife actually cared about Walter Hutcheson—she couldn't imagine herself falling for an elderly man—but after all, Heather was in a strange country, and this couldn't be a very pleasant experience for her, regardless of her feelings toward her husband. Before Elizabeth's less impulsive side could marshal any counter-arguments, she hurried up the metal steps and tapped on the door.

"Was there something you wanted?" asked a voice behind her.

Elizabeth turned, so startled that she nearly fell off the step. Heather, her pink outfit considerably the worse for wear, looked none too pleased at the prospect of a visitor. "I just came to see if there was anything I could do," Elizabeth ventured shyly.

"About what?"

"Your husband. I'm very sorry to hear about it. Can I be of any help?"

Heather's eyes narrowed. "Do you know how to drive a bloody aircraft carrier? I'd like to get myself away from here."

"I don't think you'd be allowed to. Since Dr. Hutcheson is charged with the murder—or at least being questioned— I expect that the sheriff will want to examine this camper for evidence. You might ask if you could be allowed to leave on your own." Elizabeth hesitated. "Don't you want to stay, though, in case your husband needs you?"

"I dunno. I s'pose I ought." Heather sat down on the bench at the picnic table and rumpled her blond hair as she meditated. "Hard to know what to do, really."

She isn't very old, Elizabeth thought kindly. And if she's anything like Princess Diana, she hasn't got a lot of education, either. She's probably not used to having to cope with things on her own. "Have you got any family?"

"What?"

"Someone that you could call to be with you. I don't suppose you want to be alone right now. Is all your family back in Scotland?"

"Yes. I don't want them."

"Are you sure? Someone could take a plane and be here by tomorrow, I think."

"No. I don't want them. I can take care of myself."

"Do you think you'd go back if . . ." The possibility of Walter's conviction for murder hung in the air, but Elizabeth couldn't bring herself to speak the words.

"What, back to Scotland? No chance. I'm better as I am, what with Dad on the brew."

Elizabeth nodded sympathetically. "My aunt was an alcoholic. It was very sad for the family."

Heather turned to look at her. "Right. Well, as I say, I'll be all right."

"I don't think Walter did it," Elizabeth volunteered.

"No? Why not?"

"He's just never seemed like that sort of person, I guess. Of course, the sheriff isn't going to pay any attention to character witnesses. Not when he has motive and fingerprints on his side. But maybe we could come up with some facts that will prove Walter didn't do it."

"I don't know anything."

"Okay, let me ask you a couple of questions, and let's see if we get anywhere. Did the sheriff ask you about an alibi?"

"I wasn't much of a help to him. Walter left the camper this morning before seven. He doesn't sleep too well at the best of times. And last night I can't say I was with him all the time. He went for a walk after the party. Late-night walks are a habit of his as well."

Elizabeth sighed. "That ought to prove he didn't do it. Anybody in his right mind would have provided a better alibi if he was going to commit murder."

"Not in real life, though. If you mean to do someone in, you don't think aught about it, do you?"

"You do if you don't want to get caught. The fingerprints don't make sense, either. Anybody knows not to leave fingerprints on a murder weapon. You might as well leave an autographed picture. Yet, they find his fingerprints on the hilt of the *skian dubh*. That reminds me—when was the last time you saw it?"

Heather shrugged. "I remember making sure that he brought it along. He's always so particular about his kilt and all the rest of the lot."

"Did he wear it to the party last night?"

"The one here? No. He wore it to the sherry party at Mrs. Hamilton's, but I'm nearly certain that he wore the other one after that." She smiled. "I think he felt a bit guilty about wearing it. It was a present from *her,* you know."

Elizabeth didn't want to talk about Marge, and she couldn't think of anything else to ask. Heather was right: she wasn't much help, but at least she wasn't being hysterical. "Well, if you need anything, just let me know," said Elizabeth. "I was looking for Lachlan Forsyth, actually. Do you know him?"

"The old man from the souvenir stall? I haven't seen him." Heather seemed to have lost interest in the conversation. She pulled a set of keys out of her pocket and started up the camper steps. "Thanks for stopping by."

I must ask this, thought Elizabeth, not wanting to: "Do

you want me to send Cameron over to see you?"

"I don't know," said Heather. "Perhaps I'll see him later. Not now."

Instead of the question she wanted to ask, Elizabeth said, "Heather, do you think Walter did it?"

Heather, who had been turning the key in the lock, turned and frowned at Elizabeth. "What a question to ask a wife," she said, closing the door.

Elizabeth did not find Lachlan Forsyth at any of the clan tents, nor could she find anyone who remembered seeing him. The pipe bands were giving a performance in the center field, so most of the crowd had congregated around the tents to watch the show. The mix of tartans reminded Elizabeth of the time she had melted all her crayons in her mother's best saucepan.

The Chattan tent was packed: every folding chair was occupied, and the row of coolers stretched from one tent pole to the other. Cluny was still asleep in his place of honor by the information table, but his baby-sitter, Cameron Dawson, was nowhere in sight.

"Has anybody seen Dr. Dawson?" asked Elizabeth over the whine of "MacPherson's Lament."

A man in a chair on the back row tilted his head back and wiggled his nose to keep his glasses from falling off. "Who?"

"The guy who was watching the bobcat."

"Oh. Had a speech impediment?"

Elizabeth bristled. "That," she said ominously, "was an Edinburgh prep-school accent as spoken by a Ph.D.!"

"Uh-huh. I thought he sounded funny." The man took

another sip of his drink, nearly toppling his chair in the process.

"Where is he?" said Elizabeth even more loudly.

"Whisky run," said the woman at the information table. "Jack Gilroy didn't think we had enough Scotch, so he was headed for the liquor store in Meadow Creek."

"Didn't look like he'd even make it to the parking lot," said the chair-toppler.

"Your friend offered to drive Jack to the store. He thought it would be safer."

"He hadn't had nearly as much as Jack," the man volunteered.

"I'll bet he'd had enough," Elizabeth muttered. "He's never driven on the right side of the road before. How long have they been gone?"

"Half an hour, tops."

"Okay. I'll take Cluny with me, and I'll check back in half an hour. If he comes back, keep him here!"

"Who? Jack?" the man called after her.

"No!" Elizabeth yelled back. Damned bagpipes! "The one with the speech impediment."

Elizabeth had a bit of a struggle making any progress along the path by the clan tents. For one thing, Cluny was not pleased at having his nap interrupted, and he saw no reason to cooperate during the course of the walk. His foul mood was further offset by the Saturday afternoon tourists who, now that Elizabeth did not want to be bothered with them, insisted on stopping her with questions about the Chattan mascot. Everybody wanted to pet the bobcat.

"Can we just have little Allison's picture taken with the

kitty?" asked a besotted father festooned in cameras.

Little Allison, who looked like a dismemberer of stuffed animals, was gazing at Cluny with a gleam of purpose in her piggy eyes.

"Another time," said Elizabeth sweetly. "He hasn't had all his shots." She steered the bobcat firmly away into the crowd while she tried to decide where to look for Marge. The tent or the practice meadow? She would never have spotted her at all if Somerled hadn't started to bark.

The border collie, who had been curled up by his mistress's chair in the MacDonald tent, caught the scent of strange cat and decided that the immediate world should be notified. He sprang to attention, searching the crowd of manshapes for the interloper, and spotting the bobcat a few yards away, he hunched into a menacing crouch and began to announce his discovery.

Cluny sat down with the dignity of an interrupted bishop and hissed cordially at the source of the disturbance. Fortunately, the bagpipes drowned out most of it. Before the confrontation could degenerate into a donnybrook, Marge Hutcheson sprang between them. A sharp word from her sent Somerled back to wary disapproval; Cluny was still bristling, but he no longer bothered to hiss.

"Were you looking for me?" asked Marge dryly, once peace had been restored.

Elizabeth nodded. "Nothing very important. Just thought I'd tell you how things are going."

Marge pointed her finger at the border collie. "Somerled, stay until I get back," she said sternly. She smiled at Elizabeth. "I find dogs much easier to reason with than bobcats. Now, let's take a walk while we discuss all this."

"There isn't very much to tell," Elizabeth warned her. "Nothing really dramatic. At least I found out what Colin's meeting was about."

She explained about Jerry Buchanan's zeal for a conservative tartan, and how his conversation with Colin had revealed the existence of the S.R.A. scam. By the time she reached the part about Geoffrey's impromptu initiation into the conspiracy, Marge was laughing.

"Geoffrey has created any amount of havoc," Elizabeth told her. "He's told them that Cameron was a spy, and he terrorized that poor dentist a little while ago. But he refuses to believe that any of it ties in with the murder."

Marge smiled. "What about Lachlan?"

"I can't find him. Geoffrey insists that Lachlan isn't capable of violence. Apparently it's against con-man psychology."

"And how say you, sociology major?"

"I took criminology in my sophomore year, thinking that it was going to be a fascinating course full of Jack the Ripper and blood and thunder. People always assume that; the class is packed every quarter. Actually, it's deadly dull. Mostly statistics. I don't remember a single thing."

"Well, having known Lachlan from a few seasons of festivals, I must say I don't think he's a very likely killer, either. Anyway, I don't see how he could have got hold of Walter's *skian dubh*."

"I wish I could find him. There's still a chance that one of his merry men did this for some mad reason connected with this crazy terrorist business. And they are certainly capable of a little burglary to steal a murder weapon as well."

Marge looked up. *"As well,"* she echoed. "That's pure Brit. I'll bet you didn't say that B.C."

"B.C.? Oh! Before Cameron. I guess you're right. I've been listening to his accent so hard that I must have picked up a phrase or two. Not enough, though. When Cameron met Heather, they were using a whole dictionary full of words I'd never heard of. And they'd throw in names of places (I guess) which confused me even more." She sighed. "They knew each other before."

Marge stopped walking. "Who told you that?"

"I could tell. They even had pet names for each other."

"My successor is quite the *femme fatale,* isn't she?" said Marge grimly.

"Oh, I don't know that there's anything between them anymore," Elizabeth murmured. "I couldn't tell from what they were saying. Whatever they were saying."

"Ask him."

"Ask Cameron?" Elizabeth stared. "You have to be kidding. Why, a Southern girl would tap-dance on a mine field sooner than she'd ask a loaded question like that to her . . . to Cameron."

"The way I see it, you've got two choices. You can either sit around and worry about it until you turn into a paranoid schizophrenic, or you can just up and ask him in a reasonable way. You don't have to interrogate him, Elizabeth. But it seems to me that it's your business, all things considered."

"Last night, you mean. That was pretty impulsive for a girl who usually cannot pronounce the word *yes.*" She laughed. "God, when I think of all the guys at college who wasted hours trying everything from debating tactics to bourbon. They'd never believe last night."

"Exactly. Ask him."

"Maybe. After the murder case is over. If I ever see him again."

"Ask him now," said Marge. "Some things shouldn't be put off. The case will take care of itself for that long, my girl."

"I'll see if I have the courage to do it."

"Promise you'll ask him."

Elizabeth smiled. Marge was such a wonderful person. Even with all her own worries, she could still take time to be concerned about someone else. "I promise."

CHAPTER TWELVE

He was cold. Odd that when he took a breath, the air didn't chill his nostrils and throat, but he knew it was bloody cold because his hands were numb. Where were his gloves? Wexford wouldn't half create if he caught one of his gunners without 'em. He began to feel around the dark, enclosed space for his gloves. It felt wrong somehow. He wished he could see; pitch-black it was.

"I'll just keep staring straight in front of me," he told himself, "and in a wee while the lighthouse at Buchan Ness will appear below, and that'll be the Moray Firth." If Wexford could hold the crate in the air for another quarter of an hour, they'd reach Kinloss with naught to worry about but coming down like a bloody Christmas sparkler on the runway. They could reach Kinloss, couldn't they? If not, they could always put down at Lossiemouth. Anywhere but the damned sea.

Wexford hadn't been hit, had he? He didn't like the stink crowding him out of the turret. Somebody must have bought it. Shit was the worst part of dying, as far as he could tell; poor buggers couldn't help it, of course. The numbness was more insistent now. He must have taken a hit himself, he thought.

Bagpipes? Sounds like "MacPherson's Lament." That would be a good one to tell them at the Culbin Arms in Forres tomorrow night. "The engine of my Lancaster bomber plays 'MacPherson's Lament'!" His mates were always on him about his keenness for Scottish history, but he passed it off by saying that an auctioneer has to know his stuff. He liked history well enough, and it was true that the buyers were apt to spend more for the goods if you tossed in a bit of a tale about it. A little learning might make him a bit of lucre one of these days.

Where was the bloody lighthouse? Oh, the blackout. Sod that! They weren't going to put down in the sea, were they? If he could have stood water, he'd have joined the Navy.

Flying Officer Forsyth closed his eyes. Bagpipes again. Engine trouble? As he pitched forward and fell into darkness, his last thought was that Wexford was going to ditch her in the bloody sea, and he'd never see light again.

The problem with portable toilets, thought Edwin Davis, was that there was no place to wash your hands after using the facilities. Edwin Davis was always most particular about that sort of thing. Six cakes of soap a month he went through, he'd tell his guests: a rather splendid tribute of cleanliness for one who lived alone. He shouldn't have tried that soft drink at the refreshment tent. If it hadn't been for that, he could have waited until he left the festival. As it was, he had spent a good many minutes trying to find a Port-A-John in an uncrowded area. Really, if he didn't have complete privacy, he couldn't go at all. He supposed silence was too much to ask; the bagpipe music permeated the entire mountainside.

Edwin Davis frowned at the battered blue stall set up at a precarious angle beneath a pine tree. He didn't quite like the tilt of it. He refused to consider the possibility of being trapped in a falling Port-A-John. There was no one in sight, and he was distinctly uncomfortable, so he decided to risk it. He made a mental note to reconsider attending any more outdoor festivals. Mother had always insisted that a direct descendant of Bonnie Prince Charlie ought to be present at such gatherings, but if this first experience of one was any indication of the norm, he thought they could just scrape by without him. He had found the Stewart tent easily enough, but there was something he didn't quite like in their smiling reception to his announcement of royal ancestry. Edwin could see restrained amusement beneath their politeness. They might as well accuse Mother of lying, he thought hotly.

Edwin peered closely at the handle of the portable toilet. A small lever registered "occupied" or "unoccupied," and it was now resting in the latter position. He hoped that the chemical additive was sufficiently strong to block the smell. Smells could give him the most violent headaches. Mother's powder used to, though of course he'd never mentioned it.

Taking one last deep breath of mountain air, Edwin yanked the handle of the Port-A-John and prepared to enter, but his way was blocked by the body that fell forward and landed with a soft thump on his feet. Edwin stared down at the old man in the green and blue kilt, with a detachment that was almost serene. He wasn't very heavy, really, for a corpse. Still quite distinguished-looking, in fact. The deceased didn't seem in the least embarrassed to be discovered in so undignified a place as a portable toilet. He might have died a war hero, for the noble expression he wore. After a few seconds' more contemplation beneath the glaze of shock, Edwin Davis wondered idly whether he ought to go and get someone to see about the poor old fellow. Report the death. He might as well. Upon reflection, he realized that he didn't have to go the bathroom anymore.

Walter Hutcheson had called his lawyer on the telephone in the sheriff's office. Sanderson, hauled off the golf course by his beeper, would be driving down, presumably after he'd changed into a more professional outfit. Walter was in no hurry to see him. It was quite peaceful, really, to be able to survey one's own life with the detachment that iron bars provided.

He found himself thinking about Marge for the first time in months. Really considering her, he corrected himself. She had usually flitted near the surface of his thoughts, but the accompanying reproach had kept him from focusing on her clearly. This afternoon's incident had left him shaken. Walter Hutcheson was not a man who pondered things very much—philosophy struck him as a waste of time— but even he had to see the implications of his earlier confrontation with Marge. He had forgotten about Heather completely. She had simply gone out of his head; and when the emergency overwhelmed him, he turned to Marge as naturally as a child might call on a parent. It made him very uneasy.

He had to admit that Heather would not have been very much help in a crisis. She wasn't good at independent thinking, and she seemed to have an amazing capacity for doing nothing at all—but in a very lovely way, of course. He supposed he had been a bit silly, but after all, it isn't every day one can marry into the British aristocracy. And such a beautiful girl, besides.

He looked at the bars again. Not a bad cell, really. It was clean, anyway. He hadn't seen any insects.

Walter tried to think about Heather again through the cloud of pride with which he normally saw her, but the comforting haze would not be summoned. There wasn't much aristocracy about their wedding. Justice of the peace in the courthouse soon after his divorce became final. He'd been flattered that she hadn't wanted to wait. But he should have insisted on having her people come over. He'd wanted to take her to Scotland on the honey-moon, of course, but it was winter, and Heather had insisted on Barbados. They had been married eight months now, and he had yet to meet any of her family. He wondered if she was ashamed of him; he winced at the thought. He wasn't young, that was true. At first he'd been pleased when people commented on them as a couple, even amused when she was mistaken for his daughter; just lately he'd begun to suspect that they were laughing at him.

He wished Heather were more affectionate. Perhaps

Scots weren't a very affectionate people. He'd often heard them called dour. She seemed at times to tolerate him— nothing more. But he couldn't imagine what it was she wanted. A sardonic voice in the back of his mind told him what he wanted, though: Marge. He wanted Marge.

Lightfoot MacDonald, who had been conferring with the state police, opened the door to the cell area to check on the prisoner. The doctor didn't seem like the sort of fellow to hang himself, but they took the shoelaces and all anyway, because you never knew for sure. He was sitting on his bunk now, looking two notches past sorrowful. Lightfoot liked that in a perpetrator. Remorse was something he didn't see a lot of in his business.

"How are you doing, doc?" he called out in a bracing voice. He let them save the hostility for the courtroom. His job was to catch folks and hold on to 'em, not reprimand 'em.

"Fine," said Walter, trying to smile back.

Lightfoot had exchanged his Confederate officer's uniform for a dark brown sheriff's outfit. He looked considerably more official in consequence. He pulled up a wooden kitchen chair just outside the cell and sat down with a sigh. "Been a long day," he remarked. "I get up at six when I'm taking Sorrel out with the militia. . . . My horse," he explained.

Walter nodded. "After Stonewall Jackson's mount."

Lightfoot beamed. "Imagine anybody knowing that! I wish we could have had a chat under better circumstances, Dr. Hutcheson, but as it is I need to talk about this situation out at the festival. That is, if you're ready

171

to make a statement."

Walter considered it. Sanderson would be seething if he didn't wait for legal counsel. Might even refuse the case. Anyway, there wasn't much he could say past, "I didn't do it." He thought he knew who did, but that wasn't something he was prepared to discuss. It didn't make any sense, anyway. He considered letting them convict him without a struggle, and going off to a quiet prison. Marge would write to him; he was sure of that.

"I'm sorry, Sheriff. I mustn't discuss anything until my lawyer arrives."

Lightfoot nodded. "Everybody watches television these days. Okee-fine. But I don't mind telling you that this case is downright peculiar. Fingerprints, no alibi, good obvious motive. That's great for the beer joint stabbings I have to contend with, but if M.D.s don't have any more sense than that . . ."

Walter felt the same way. Not only was it a frame, it was an insult to his intelligence. It was so obvious that they might even make a jury see it. He didn't much care, though. He was tired.

Lightfoot had pulled out a notepad and was about to launch into further arguments when the door to the outer office opened and Merle Fentress peeked around it. "Call for you, Sheriff," he said in meaningful tones.

"Who?"

"Festival people again."

"Now what?" asked Lightfoot, pushing back his chair.

"Another murder, they reckon."

Lightfoot glanced at the prisoner, and then edged past the deputy into the office. "Damnit!" he muttered. "Never mind the battle reenactment. This case may outlast the war!"

Lightfoot eased the patrol car off the state highway and turned up the road to Glencoe Park. He felt a spasm of irritation as he drove past the posters announcing the Highland games, and then the Civil War reenactment. Damnit, there ought not to be more bodies the week before the battle than there were during it. He wondered if Dr. Hutcheson had disposed of this one about the same time as the first murder, or whether there was another killer at large. The coroner ought to be able to help with that one. Maybe his hunch was right, and the doctor had been framed: that was easier to swallow than the mass-murderer theory.

Lightfoot narrowed his eyes. What in blazes was wrong with that sports car up ahead of him? Other than its driving on the wrong side of the road. Oh, hellfire, thought Lightfoot, the drunks are getting in on the act. He flipped on his flasher and eased up toward the offending vehicle with catlike smoothness.

After a few seconds in which the two occupants seemed to confer, the car pulled over on the grass. Lightfoot slid his Dodge in behind them and made notes of the description and license plate. Having thus given the offenders time to stew about their predicament, he slid out of the patrol car and strolled toward the blue MG.

"Well, it has the bloody steering wheel on the correct side," the driver was saying to his companion. "It was a perfectly natural—what did you say? Well, I'd like to see your performance under similar circumstances!"

"Step out of the car, please, sir," purred Lightfoot in his

official voice. His eyes widened when he recognized the driver of the sports car. "Well, hello, Scotty! Is this a spy car with cannons mounted on the fender?"

Cameron Dawson was annoyed. "Save it, Sheriff! I have spent a good hour nursemaiding this . . . this . . ."

Lightfoot peered in at the passenger. "Pretty far gone, isn't he?"

"Yes, and he wanted to drive."

The sheriff shook his head. "You reckon he could'a done much worse?"

"As I was trying to tell him: it was a perfectly natural mistake. In Britain we drive on the left side of the road, and this is a British car, so—"

"Yeah, but it's an American road, doncha know," Lightfoot drawled. "Can I see your license, please, Scotty?"

With a sigh of martyrdom, Cameron reached into his hip pocket and pulled out a clear plastic case. "British driving license," he said in answer to the sheriff's puzzled look.

Lightfoot took the document with a frown of suspicion. He pulled the work paper out of the plastic case, looked down the length of it and read a few lines, his lips moving. "Expires in . . . 2025! Do they mean the year?"

"That's right."

"That's crazy. And there's no picture of you on here, either. And most critical, it is not a Virginia driver's license."

"It's good for thirty days in this country," Cameron informed him.

"Yeah, I'd like to give you thirty days for it," Lightfoot grunted. "And another sixty for reckless driving; but as it happens I have another murder to contend with, so I do not have time to deal with you. Why don't I just follow you along into the park so you can't do any more English things on the way? Then you can stick around while I investigate."

"Sheriff, I've tried to explain to you that I am not—"

"Or I could write you up, and radio for someone to come and get you."

Cameron's lips tightened. "Right, Sheriff. I'll meet you at the car park."

The county rescue squad, already on duty for the festival, had cordoned off the area and were standing watch over the body when Lightfoot MacDonald and his British colleague arrived. They had covered Lachlan Forsyth's body in a sheet, but the scene otherwise was just as they had found it.

Lightfoot squinted in the late-afternoon sun. The military practice should be breaking up by now. He had half a mind to give Blevins a call on the mobile phone, but he resisted the impulse. Twentieth-century business came first. The coroner should be on his way back, and wouldn't he be a ray of sunshine after being hauled out twice in a day?

The sheriff knelt down and gently lifted the sheet. "Another stabbing," he grunted. "Anybody know who this one belonged to?"

The rescue-squad leader, squatting on his heels near the Port-A-John, said, "That festival chairman seemed to think it was his."

"His?"

"Sorry. Belonged to the deceased himself, I aimed to say."

Lightfoot looked up at Cameron Dawson. "You know

anything about this?"

"Just the identity. That was Lachlan Forsyth. He was a Scot," said Cameron quietly.

"Damn! Not your spies again?"

"He was the organizer of the—the fraud, I guess you'd call it. I don't see why anyone would have killed him for it. Unless they were annoyed at having been taken in. He got a lot of money out of them, I suppose."

Lightfoot slid the sheet back into place. He had been a distinguished-looking old fellow; that kind makes the best con man, he thought sardonically. He didn't like the idea of a murder unrelated to the first one—because this was an unlikely convention spot for killers—but life didn't always follow the rules of good taste or common sense, so Lightfoot was keeping an open mind. He turned back to the rescue-squad leader. "My people will be along directly to take over. Meanwhile, keep everybody away from here. I'm going to talk to folks, starting with the lucky so-and-so who found the body. Have somebody notify me when the coroner arrives."

James Stuart McGowan had been assigning tartans and dispensing plaid woolens with the authority of the Lord Lyon of Scotland. It was very easy, once you got the hang of it. He had already made enough money to buy two *skian dubhs,* if you counted the markup he was pocketing; he thought about slipping that money back into the till. If Lachlan found out how solvent he was, it would either cause awkward questions, or he would sell him the dagger and cancel the apprenticeship. If he took the money with him, and Babs and Stewie found it, things could get even stickier. They would assume that he was dealing drugs and ship him off to a shrink with an earth-tone office.

He supposed that he had earned the money, really. He had spent half the time running the stall alone. Lachlan was taking some break this time. It must have been three hours, and Jimmy—who hadn't eaten since lunch—was beginning to miss him. He helped himself to another Penguin bar from the food section. He wondered if he could find an elderly lady both sympathetic and dumb enough to bring him a shandy from the refreshment tent.

The Maid of the Cat was approaching the stall. He smiled thinking of the way he had conned her into buying a scarf. It ought not to be too hard to get a shandy out of her, he decided. But what was she looking so grim about?

"Hello," he said, tossing the foil candy wrapper into the trash bag. "What can I sell you this time?"

Elizabeth didn't smile back. "What's your name?" she asked gently.

"Jimmy," he said warily, not liking her tone.

"And was Mr. Forsyth your grandfather, perhaps?"

"Perhaps. My grandmother doesn't confide in me."

Her sympathetic look turned to exasperation, which Jimmy found much easier to abide. "Now what's this all about?"

She hesitated. "Are your parents around, dear?"

He shrugged. "Someplace. They don't count, though. You'd better talk to me. What is it about Lachlan? Something about those clowns he was always whispering with?"

Elizabeth sighed. Even under the pressure of a double murder, she thought someone more official than she should have been delegated to tell the little boy. "I'm sorry," she said. "He's been killed. They found him a little while ago."

Jimmy stared at her. She was watching him anxiously as if she expected him to start howling. People never seemed to know much about kids; something must happen to your memory when you passed thirteen. He'd often wondered about it. Now, what was it that he was avoiding thinking about that made him consider all that? Oh, yes. Lachlan was dead.

"How?" he asked, in the tones of one seeking information.

"Just like the first victim, I'm afraid."

"Stabbed with a *skian dubh*."

"Yes. Oh, but you mustn't think about it. I'm sure your parents—"

Jimmy looked in the glass case. He'd been too busy all morning to notice. The *skian dubh* was gone. The old man must have taken it with him. For protection, of course. He'd never have it now, which absolved him from asking himself if he could possibly want it.

The girl was still droning on. Something about locating his "Mommy and Daddy." As Jimmy pushed past her out of the stall, heading at a dead run for the woods, he yelled back at her, "Just sod off!"

That phrase—his only legacy from Lachlan Forsyth.

From the outside table in the refreshment tent, Elizabeth could keep an eye on the path to the parking lot. Cameron should be coming back anytime now. She hoped she hadn't missed him when she went to talk to the little boy; but when she realized that everyone had overlooked him, she didn't feel that she had any choice. She leaned down and offered the rest of her sausage roll to Cluny, who took it with the air of performing a favor. Really, she had to stop eating this British pastry before she started receiving offers to play lineman for Green Bay.

"Hello," said Marge Hutcheson, edging her way through the crowd with a cup of coffee in her hand. "Mind if I join you?"

"Hello, Marge," said Elizabeth. "I was thinking about coming to look for you. I guess you've heard what happened."

"To Lachlan Forsyth? Yes. Too bad, wasn't it?"

"I suppose it clears Walter?"

"I expect so. Depends on when he was killed, don't you think? So you never got to question him."

Elizabeth sighed. "No. I probably wouldn't have been able to come up with the right questions anyway."

Marge patted her hand. "Don't sell yourself short," she said kindly. "The murderer will probably turn out to be someone we've never even heard of. Somebody crazy, perhaps. Why don't you forget all about the case, and get things straight with that sexy Scot of yours?"

Sexy! It's amazing how my brain is turning to mush, Elizabeth thought. Instead of wanting to reconsider the murder case, the first thing I think of is whether I would quibble with that adjective. The sexiest thing about Cameron is that he doesn't seem aware of it at all. I practically had to drag him . . .

She interrupted this pleasant reverie when she noticed someone looming over the table. "Hello, Geoffrey. What do you want?"

Geoffrey sighed. "Oddly enough, I want the damned cat. I was just walking around in the woods, turning over a few ideas for set design in my head, when I hear the damnedest noise from some rocks. Rather like a hiccoughing ferret."

"Oh, dear," said Elizabeth, who had learned to ignore Geoffrey's powers of description. "Was it a little boy?"

"Yes. An odious child who has been manning a souvenir stall. But he seems quite distressed. I gather he's grieving for one of the murder victims, which is a refreshing novelty."

Elizabeth winced. "Yes. His name is Jimmy. But why do you want the bobcat?"

"Because I want to take his mind off his troubles. It will do him good to have another soulless creature under his charge, and you don't want the cat anymore, surely, since you have other prey to stalk. Correct?"

Elizabeth handed over the leash. "Make sure he takes good care of Cluny!" she warned. "Bobcats can be dangerous animals."

"So can ten-year-old boys," Geoffrey assured her.

As they watched him move away, gingerly leading the Chattan mascot, Marge remarked, "You know, sometimes I think that cousin of yours is almost human."

"Almost," Elizabeth agreed.

CHAPTER THIRTEEN

Elizabeth caught her breath. Here goes, she thought. Cameron Dawson and Sheriff MacDonald were walking back together on the path that led to the parking area. She wanted to see him so badly. She wished he were in China. She wanted to run and hold him, right in front of everybody. She was scared to death of him. And mostly, she kept forgetting to breathe.

Before she could make up her mind to lose herself in the crowd at the counter, he had caught sight of her and waved, smiling. Elizabeth waved back, feeling the hot flush in her cheeks. Damn you, anyway, Cameron, she thought. You're like a bloody baby giraffe: you're trampling me and you don't even know it.

Bloody! Even the words were his.

He had said something to the sheriff—who had gone into the hospitality tent—and now he was coming toward her as innocently as a falling cable car. I love you so much, she thought; please get the hell away from me. I don't want to live through the next five minutes, and you're damn sure not going to enjoy it either, kid.

He still had about twenty yards to traverse, during which time she tried psyching herself into indifference. Sometimes he hardly even knows I'm there, she told herself; he talks to me—at me—as if he were cleaning out his mind. And when I try to tell him things, he replies with something so off-the-wall that he can't have been listening. I wonder if he even takes women seriously. I might as well be a seal, sometimes.

This line of reasoning might have worked if it had not been overlaid with a ton of subjectivity, all in the offender's favor. The part of Elizabeth's mind reserved for the defense replied with a soft-focus video memory of the night before, accompanied by a sound track of a country song: "Loving you feels just like coming home."

Oh, well, she thought, when my level of reasoning is reduced to quoting country music, I might as well throw myself in front of a Mack truck. A *Mac*Truck, she thought ruefully. And here it comes.

Cameron Dawson, still a bit edgy from having to suffer fools gladly for the last hour or so, was blissfully unaware that he personified disaster. "Hello," he said, still smiling. "I nearly got myself thrown in jail just now. I tried to do a good deed, mind you, and keep a bloody drunk off the road by giving him a lift, and that sheriff wanted to put me away."

"I expect you were on the brew yourself," Elizabeth replied, remembering Heather's phrase.

Cameron blinked. "What? No, I don't think so. Dr. Campbell is dead, so I expect I'll be allowed to go ahead with my seal research."

"What does that have to do with drinking?"

"We weren't talking about drinking," Cameron pointed out. " 'On the brew' means unemployed."

Elizabeth shrugged. Heather couldn't have meant it that way. British nobles did not have unemployed fathers. (Did they?) Apparently the nobles had their own version of slang. She was too polite to mention this to Cameron, though.

"I've just been up with the sheriff, looking at poor Mr. Forsyth. He was a very nice fellow; it's a great pity." He looked at her. "Is that sort of thing usual in this country?"

"Two murders a day?" murmured Elizabeth. "Not usually in one's immediate vicinity." She did not offer any further topics of conversation, which was most unusual for Elizabeth, who often talked to avoid having to communicate.

"Is anything wrong?" asked Cameron finally.

"We need to talk," Elizabeth said quietly.

Oh shit, thought Cameron. He may have only been in the States for a matter of hours, but cultural gap or no, when a woman says, "We have to talk," there's a storm brewing. "Okay," he said pleasantly. "Want to walk a bit while we're doing it?"

Elizabeth nodded. In the direction of a cliff, she thought. "It isn't really very important," she murmured when they were out of the festival crowd. "Just something I thought I probably ought to ask you."

Cameron was silent for a moment, and his ears had turned noticeably redder. "Fire away, ma'am," he said, still as calm as ever. *It isn't very important* was another danger sign.

Elizabeth looked at the soft green mountains couching the sky like so many overstuffed sofas. Appalachian mountains, she thought: you can't see them for the trees. And we are just like them: everything is soft and covered up by layers of politeness and caution. I couldn't say anything straight out if my life depended on it. She wondered what the mountains were like in Scotland.

"I realize that last night probably didn't mean anything," she began slowly.

Cameron didn't look at her. "I don't know," he said carefully. "It did to me."

"Well, I just wanted you to know that you don't have to keep spending time with me if you don't want to. If you'd rather be with somebody else, I'll understand."

"Someone else? I've spent the last two hours with a drunk and a sheriff who thinks I'm a spy. Is that your idea of competition?"

"No. I thought there was someone else here that you

might want to be with. And I guess she needs you more than I do, now that her husband—"

Cameron thought it all through very carefully. *She* and *husband* and Elizabeth's look of moist-eyed nobility. He took a wild guess. "Are you talking about Heather?"

"I know it's none of my business," Elizabeth murmured. "It was pretty obvious that you knew her back in Scotland, and I thought you might still be in love with her."

The rest of her carefully planned speech might have rivaled Sydney Carton's address from the guillotine, but she didn't get to deliver it. It would have spoiled the emotional content of the scene, what with Cameron sitting on the ground laughing. Elizabeth was confused. There is something here that I'm missing, she told herself. It wasn't the kind of laughing that one associates with guilt or embarrassment. He was laughing just as if she had said something incredibly stupid.

"I suppose it's all over now as far as you're concerned, but I'm not sure about her. She probably should have someone she likes with her right now. Oh, maybe you should call the British embassy. After all, she is the niece of the Duke of Rothesay, and perhaps they'd send someone to advise her."

Cameron, still grinning, looked up at her. "What did you say?"

"That the British embassy might send someone—"

"No. Before that. She's what?"

"I don't know what her title is. Walter just says that she's the niece of the Duke of Rothesay. He's been bragging about it all weekend. Of course, you'd know, wouldn't you? What is the correct thing to call her?"

His eyes narrowed. "I think impostor would just about cover it," he said evenly.

"What?"

"Everyone kept telling me she had a title, and I thought she was claiming to be a cousin of a life-peer. That was just barely possible. She wouldn't have a title, of course, but I put it down to American generalization. I wouldn't have thought she could get anyone to fall for this rubbish, though."

"What rubbish?"

"Do you know who the Duke of Rothesay is?"

Elizabeth shook her head.

"It's the Scottish title for the Prince of Wales. In other words, the present Bonnie Prince Charlie."

"Walter must have got it wrong, then. Maybe it's an earl with a similar title."

Cameron patted the grass beside him. "Sit down. We're going to talk about this long-lost love of mine." When Elizabeth had settled beside him, being careful not to get too close—she still wasn't sure about all of it—Cameron said, "All right. Granted that Heather and I are both Scottish. But do you notice any differences between us?"

Discarding all the time-wasting smart answers, Elizabeth said, "Well, her accent. And you don't seem to use the same words much."

"Very good, ma'am. What about her accent?"

"It's so cute. Yours sounds sort of BBC, but hers is really Scottish."

"Bloody hell!" muttered Cameron, shaking his head. "I see how she's pulled it off then." He sighed. "Heather's accent, my dear, is perfectly normal if you happen to be from the Gorbals. That's the slum area of Glasgow."

"Are you sure?"

"Of course I'm sure! And I let her know it, too, when we were at that party of theirs. I suppose that was why she went out of her way to be insulting."

Elizabeth tried to remember the gibberish they'd been talking at the party. "Something about a Ming bird," she said at last. "I remember thinking about Chinese art."

Cameron sighed. "She said the bobcat stank. A ming is a bad smell." He paused, thinking how to word the next bit. "And a bird is a girl."

Elizabeth scowled. "Why that . . . What else did she say?"

"Let's see . . . Right after she made that remark, I decided to test her ladyship. So I said—"

"What was that Bella . . . something?"

"Oh, that. I was talking about schools. She claimed to have gone to Park, which is an exclusive girls' school in Glasgow, and I knew that was rubbish. So I said, Bella-houston."

"What's that?"

"A public park. The only park she could get into, I meant."

"You also asked her about a farm, didn't you?"

"A farm? Oh, I must have asked, did she come from a dear green place."

"Isn't that a farm?"

"No. In Gaelic the word for dear green place is Glasgow."

Elizabeth brightened. "You know Gaelic?"

"About a dozen words."

So Lachlan had been right about that. "She's been calling you a Sloane Ranger, whatever that is."

"Yes. I think you have another word for it in America. Preppy?"

"How would she know that?"

Cameron smiled. "Can you spot American ones?"

"Of course! I see what you mean. You spotted her by her accent and vocabulary, and she knew you for the same reasons." She looked suspicious. "But you must have known her before, because you had pet names for each other."

"We did? What?"

Elizabeth was never going to forget those. "Jimmy and Senga," she said promptly.

He laughed. "Do you have a name you call somebody when you don't know their name?"

She thought about it. "Buddy? Like 'Hey, Buddy, watch it!'"

"Exactly. We say Jimmy. And Senga is . . ." He hesitated.

"Is what?"

"Agnes spelled backwards. It's really used as a name." He smiled. "But not by the nieces of dukes."

Elizabeth nodded slowly. "Like Ethel-May. So you knew that Heather was a phony aristocrat. Who else would know?"

"Any Scot." Cameron shrugged. "Anyone who knew much about Scotland."

"Lachlan Forsyth?"

"None better."

"And the fact that the Duke of Rothesay is Prince Charles. Anybody who knew a lot about genealogy and Scottish traditions would know that."

"I expect so. They mentioned it during the royal wedding, which is how I happened to know. Watched it on the TV at the lab."

"What's a baby sham?"

"What does that have to do with anything? Babycham is a drink that you might get at the pub . . . for a Senga."

Elizabeth nodded slowly. "Then Colin Campbell knew."

"Of course. I didn't say anything about her passing herself off as a snob. It wasn't any business of mine, and I certainly didn't think you'd be jumping to the daft conclusions you did. Anybody could see she hated me." He scowled. "She called me a *toffee-nose*."

Elizabeth kissed him on the cheek. "I think you have a beautiful nose," she said. "And the rest of you is pretty adorable, too, but right now we have to go and find the sheriff." She stood up and brushed the grass from her skirt.

"What?" said Cameron.

"We have a murder to solve. And once that's out of the way, you can get back to biology." Seeing his bewilderment, she added, "Not seals and porpoises."

Sheriff Lightfoot MacDonald, already in a black mood at having to spell out *skian dubh* on umpty-million police forms, scowled at the two young people in front of him— holding hands, yet! "I ain't no goddamn justice of the peace," he rumbled.

"No, Sheriff," said Elizabeth politely, letting go of Cameron's hand. "We brought you some information about the murder."

"We've solved it!" Cameron chimed in.

Lightfoot's headache went up a notch. "One of you confessing?" he drawled.

Elizabeth and Cameron looked at each other. "Let me explain," she said. "You help me out on the cultural points."

Lightfoot looked at his watch and yawned.

"I guess to understand the murders, you'd have to know about Scottish-Americans," Elizabeth began.

"We aren't all crazy," grumbled the descendant of Flora MacDonald.

"No," Cameron agreed. "But most of the ones here don't know much about Scotland in the present century."

"They don't even want to. They're perfectly happy rooting around for ancestors who might have held the Bonnie Prince's horse, or been a third cousin of someone with a title. Titles are very glamorous to Americans. So when Heather McSkye—"

"Which couldn't be her real name," Cameron put in. "McSkye, indeed!"

"—When Heather claimed to be the niece of a duke, it just bowled poor Walter over."

"So?" growled Lightfoot, hoping this was leading somewhere soon.

"So he divorced his wife and married *her,* which I'm practically sure he wouldn't have done otherwise. He might have been attracted to her, but I think it would have passed otherwise. She wasn't a very nice person."

"She was a right bloody bitch."

"Which brings us to another not-very-nice person," said Elizabeth, ignoring him. "Colin Campbell. He was obsessed with Scottish traditions, and ancestry, and all the rest of it. So when he heard who Heather claimed to be, he

189

knew she was a phony."

"Why?" asked Lightfoot, interested.

Elizabeth explained about the Duke of Rothesay, and Heather's real background as evidenced by her accent and manner. "Cameron knew she was a fake right away," she said.

The sheriff looked over at Dr. Dawson. "Then how come you're not dead, boy?"

"I think it's because I let her know that I wasn't interested in giving the game away," said Cameron slowly.

"I think it's because he hasn't been near her since, and he hasn't been alone all day," said Elizabeth. "Anyway, Colin Campbell would have been delighted to make a fool of Walter in front of the whole festival. He already had a score to settle with him about that land business."

The sheriff nodded. "I know about that. Go on."

"He told Walter that he wanted to call a meeting about a fraud, and he meant Lachlan Forsyth and the S.R.A., but then he met Heather. I'm sure he was planning to put her in as Fraud: Part Two, and she overheard about the meeting and may have known what he planned. He let her know he was on to her."

"How?"

"He congratulated her on having a new baby cousin. Prince Charles and Princess Diana have a new baby, of course. So that she knew that he realized who the Duke of Rothesay was."

"So she killed him to keep the secret?"

"Yes. She had just as much access to Walter's *skian dubh* as he did."

"That's the part that don't make sense," Lightfoot

remarked. "If a woman kills somebody in order to keep her husband from being disillusioned with her, then why would she go and use his weapon—marked with his fingerprints—and get him arrested for the crime?"

Elizabeth thought it over. "I don't think Heather loved Walter. She didn't want him to divorce her, but that was for economic reasons."

"If he was sent to prison for the crime, she would have control of all his money, wouldn't she?" asked Cameron. "A lot of money and no husband might be preferable to having money and one you didn't care for, especially if you were always having to worry about your lies coming out. Getting him sent away might have been a great relief for her."

Elizabeth nodded. "I agree. I think she went to see Colin Campbell early this morning and stabbed him—before he could call that board meeting and ruin her scheme."

"What about murder number two?"

"Another source of danger," said Elizabeth. "Lachlan would have known she was a fake as well."

"He'd have got it faster than I did," said Cameron. "He knew which part of Edinburgh I came from straight after I'd met him."

"Blackmail?" asked Lightfoot.

"Maybe," sighed Elizabeth. "But he didn't approach her until after Walter was arrested, did he? I don't know. I'd like to think that he didn't want the wrong person convicted for the murder, and that he wanted her to give herself up."

"Blackmail," said Cameron.

"This isn't evidence," Lightfoot warned them.

"Tell Walter the truth about her," Elizabeth advised. "I'll bet he knows that she took the *skian dubh,* and that she wasn't around early this morning. You'll have all the evidence you need."

"You'll give her the third degree, anyway, won't you, Sheriff?" asked Cameron.

Lightfoot turned to Elizabeth. "Get him out of here."

She smiled. "I bet you'll be glad to get this case out of the way."

"Yes, ma'am." He was dialing his mobile telephone. "Hello, Merle? Bring Dr. Hutcheson with you out to Glencoe Park. Yeah, we got a new development. Quick as you can. Out." The sheriff put the phone back on his belt. "Yep, I sure will be glad to finish this case. We need to get this park back to normal, too."

"For the Civil War reenactment?"

"Right. I still got practices to schedule. And then after that, I'll have to come back up here next weekend, because the park is being used by the SCA."

"Is that the group that dresses up in armor and holds jousting tournaments? Those people are crazy," sniffed the Chattan Maid of the Cat.

"I agree with you there, ma'am," said Confederate Colonel Lightfoot MacDonald.

Elizabeth found Marge Hutcheson in the practice meadow with Somerled and the rookie ducks. The feathered troops had calmed down considerably since they realized that they were not intended to be puppy chow, and they were now happily marching through concrete pipes and up little ramps, at the border collie's bidding.

"We may be able to do the trials again tomorrow," Marge remarked. "These brutes are nearly manageable now."

Elizabeth nodded. The collie seemed in perfect control again, sliding across the field like the planchette of a Ouija board. "I came to tell you that the case is solved," she said quietly.

"Someone confessed?" asked Marge.

"No. Cameron and I figured it out." She hesitated, wondering what effect this was going to have. Marge didn't need more complications in her life. She hoped this wouldn't be one. "It was Heather."

Marge pulled a cigarette out of the pack in her pocket. "Tell me about it," she said.

Elizabeth explained about the Duke of Rothesay, and the rest of their deductions. "The sheriff brought Walter back, and we told him the truth. He had known, of course, that she was the logical person to have taken his *skian dubh*."

"Didn't want to believe it, of course," muttered Marge.

"He did, though," said Elizabeth. "When they confronted her with the evidence, she confessed, but she's trying to say that Colin attacked her, and that it was self-defense."

"Hardly twice in one day," said Marge dryly. "You say Walter is back?"

"Yes. I think he's in the camper. The sheriff took Heather away. Walter says that the lawyer can take over her case, since he's on his way down, anyway." Elizabeth hesitated again.

"What else?"

"Well . . . Walter wants to see you."

"Does he?" Marge smiled. "I expect he does. Poor Walter. He's had a roller-coaster of a year, hasn't he?" She brushed a lock of hair from her forehead. "I'd better go and see about him."

"Are you sure?" asked Elizabeth.

Marge Hutcheson smiled. "Oh, yes, Elizabeth. You have to be forgiving in this world. And I think it's best for Walter. Tell him I'll be along when I get things packed up here."

CHAPTER FOURTEEN

What a happy ending, thought Elizabeth as she walked back to the festival area. The bagpipes were playing "Scotland the Brave," and she almost felt like dancing. She was sure that Marge and Walter would get back together again, and she was glad for Marge. And as for herself—the case was over, and there was still another night and half-day of the festival to spend with Cameron. The fleeting thoughts that she spared for Heather were intended to reflect sympathy for her, that she should have resorted to murder over something that should have been so trivial; but Elizabeth was not very good at empathizing with people she disliked. She caught herself gloating, and dismissed Heather from further consideration.

Elizabeth found it easier to be sorry about Lachlan Forsyth. He had been a charming old scoundrel—like Long John Silver—and she regretted his passing. She patted the pocket where she had put the note he left her. Looking toward the souvenir stall, she expected to see it covered in canvas, awaiting removal, but it was surrounded by customers, just as usual. What on earth, she thought.

When she had elbowed her way past a dozen people,

Elizabeth found two clerks doing a brisk business: Jimmy and Geoffrey. They were edging around each other, making change and reaching for paper bags with the ease of long-practiced co-workers. "What are you doing in here?" Elizabeth demanded as Geoffrey went by.

"Fleecing this little plaid flock," Geoffrey purred. "And Cluny is right over here in his basket. He makes a great crowd-attractor, does Cluny."

"Why are you doing this?"

Geoffrey lowered his voice. "The money we make will go toward the funeral expenses," he said quietly. "Jimmy wants it this way."

Elizabeth nodded. "Well, I'm glad I found you. I wanted you to know that I solved the case." She tossed her head in satisfaction.

"Did you?"

"Yes! It was Heather. Come out of there for a minute and I'll tell you about it."

Geoffrey listened patiently while Elizabeth gave him a full account of the brilliance of her deductions, with a little credit to Cameron for providing all the keys to the puzzle. "It was very simple, really," she told him. "I knew that Walter would never want Heather if he knew the truth, because he'd think she'd made a fool of him. Heather must have known that, too, of course. And there was no way to shut up Colin Campbell, short of murder. You know what a tartar he was."

"Very interesting," said Geoffrey politely.

Elizabeth looked up at him suspiciously. "You needn't think I'm wrong," she snapped. "The sheriff agreed with me, and once he got Walter back here and confronted

Heather with it, she confessed."

"You are to be commended," said Geoffrey gently.

Elizabeth looked embarrassed. "Oh, it isn't just that. The best part is that Marge and Walter are getting back together. At least, I'll bet they do. She's down in the practice meadow now, but she's going to go and see him in a little while. I'll bet you anything they'll be at next year's festival as a married couple again. I'm really happy for Marge. She's such a wonderful person that she deserves some happiness."

"And thanks to you, she shall have it," said Geoffrey, more courteously than ever.

Elizabeth was puzzled. "Is anything wrong, Geoffrey? You haven't said anything nasty in several minutes."

"No, no," he murmured. "I was simply overcome by your brilliance. Now go and find Cameron before some other American girl decides to major in international relations."

When she had gone, Geoffrey stood for a few moments more, lost in thought. Finally he told Jimmy that he was taking a break, and strolled off in the direction of the practice meadow.

Somerled had finished his herding exercise, and was just shooing the last of the platoon back into the wooden box, when Geoffrey strolled up, hands in his pockets, to watch the proceedings.

"I hope you haven't come to help," growled Marge, shutting the lid.

Geoffrey shook his head. "No. My cousin tells me that she has just solved the murder case, and that all is now well again."

Marge nodded. "Elizabeth is a clever girl."

"Elizabeth is also a trusting girl," Geoffrey replied. "And sometimes not as clever as she thinks."

"She solved the case, didn't she?"

"You know, I wondered about that," said Geoffrey. "It all seemed so convenient. Elizabeth kept telling me how she would run around and question this person or that person, and she always learned something useful. It was almost as if someone knew where to send her. And then when I heard that you had urged her to talk to Cameron about their little misunderstanding, and lo! That little interview solved the whole case. That is not detection, madam, it is stage-managing. I believe the congratulations are due to you."

"I kept out of it." Marge shrugged.

"Yes, I know you did. You let Elizabeth do all the visible sleuthing to incriminate Heather and then you stood back and let Walter Hutcheson fall into your lap. No one could ever blame you for what happened."

"I had to," said Marge, beginning a new cigarette. "No matter how guilty Heather was, if I had been the one to implicate her, Walter could never have come back to me. People would say I had manipulated all of it."

"No doubt," Geoffrey agreed. "By the way, did Heather happen to do it?"

"Oh, yes," said Marge. "I saw her." She grinned at Geoffrey's look of astonishment. "Early this morning I was going over to see Colin Campbell, and I saw Heather go into his camper. I wondered what that was about, and of course I wasn't going in while she was there, so I waited. She left a few minutes later, practically running, and I went in and found him."

"You didn't tell anybody?" asked Geoffrey. "No, sorry! Of course not; mustn't get involved."

"I wanted what was best for Walter," said Marge. "She had spoiled enough. I knew I could find a way to trap her without getting involved personally."

"Someone else died because you waited."

Marge blew a bit of smoke in the direction of the festival. "I didn't foresee that—or Walter's arrest. But that was their lookout. Men have their own way too much in this world, and women are expected to be meek, even when being trampled. We get back as best we can."

"I see. So you manipulated Elizabeth into playing detective, and you saw that she solved the case."

"It wasn't difficult, since I was working backwards."

"Yes, of course. Did you know why she'd done it?"

"That she was an impostor? Certainly. It was I who told Colin Campbell about her in the first place. Elizabeth told me the Duke of Rothesay nonsense, and I knew that Colin would ferret that out."

"I saw you tell him," said Geoffrey, remembering. "I was replacing the ducks in the wooden box."

"Quite right."

"So, in a way, you arranged for the murders to happen."

"Hardly that." Marge smiled. "I didn't tell the little bitch to murder people. But it was over for her anyway. Colin would have reveled in exposing that little fraud at the festival."

"Quite a blow to Walter, public humiliation," Geoffrey observed.

Marge shrugged. "What of it? Walter deserved a good

deal of public humiliation. I owe him about a year's worth."

Geoffrey looked grave. "My cousin idolizes you."

She smiled bitterly. "Going to tell her?"

"For the sake of her illusions, no," said Geoffrey. "I happen to like innocence. It's so rare these days."

Cameron was talking about Scottish food, but most of the lecture was wasted on Elizabeth, who was busy planning the rest of the evening. She looked down at the sausage roll on her plate and at the little plastic knife and fork she had been given to eat with. Now, what had Lachlan told her to do? Cut with her other hand?

"Have you ever had trifle?" Cameron was saying. "I wonder if you can get it in this country?"

"I don't know." All his *e*'s sound like *a*'s, she thought. *Get* becomes *gate*. I must practice that; it's so cute.

"Maybe the people who run this refreshment stand have a catalogue or something . . ."

Elizabeth looked up. "So you're going to stay?" she asked.

"I don't know. Maybe. Dr. Carson and I are going to meet with some of the foundation people on Tuesday to see if I can continue my seal research. I don't think anyone will really want a study on the Chesapeake Bay monster, now that Dr. Campbell is gone."

Elizabeth blushed. "I'd be glad to show you around the university."

"Thank you," said Cameron, equally shyly.

It seems funny to be strangers still, she thought to herself. In one way, we're as close as possible, and yet there is so much we don't know about each other. I wonder if he likes country music? She watched for a moment as he deftly carved his pastry, holding the knife and fork in either hand.

She looked down at her sausage roll. Left hand, huh?

How hard could it be? Picking up the knife gingerly, she angled it at the hard pastry and began to saw. The plastic blade snapped in two.

Elizabeth shook her head. She slid the bit of paper bearing Lachlan's scrawl out of her dress pocket and studied the words. Leaning across the table, she said carefully, *"Tha gaol agam ort."*

Cameron looked puzzled. "What does that mean?"

She sighed. "It means I can't use a knife with my left hand."

Center Point Publishing
600 Brooks Road • PO Box 1
Thorndike ME 04986-0001 USA

(207) 568-3717

US & Canada:
1 800 929-9108